LIFE HAPPENS

Thank you for your support.

Caroline R.

LIFE HAPPENS

Caroline Reber

This is a work of fiction. Names, characters, organizations, places, events, and incidents are either products of the author's imagination or are used fictitiously.

Copyright © 2017 Caroline Reber
All rights reserved.

No part of this book may be reproduced, or stored in a retrieval system, or transmitted in any form or by any means, electronic, mechanical, photocopying, recording, or otherwise, without express written permission of the publisher.

Published by Quill, an imprint of Inkshares, Inc.,
San Francisco, California
www.inkshares.com

Cover design by Xavier Comas

© DesignPicsInc/Depositphotos
© 3213080_clashot/Depositphotos
© Vladimir Gjorgiev/Depositphotos
© Ysbrand Cosijn/Depositphotos
Image Composite: Coverkitchen

ISBN: 9781942645122
e-ISBN: 9781942645306
Library of Congress Control Number: 2016941593

First edition

Printed in the United States of America

This book is dedicated to anyone who is overcome with a big challenge. Focus on what you can control, for it is where you will find your strength.

I am not what happened to me, I
am what I choose to become.

—C. G. Jung

INTRODUCTION

Do you sometimes feel like you're running through life? The days slip through your fingers quicker than water, and you are not sure how to slow things down? It's not necessarily bad, just a bit too fast.

I used to live that way and probably still would if life had not shaken me from the ground up.

At first, I spent a lot of time being sad, mad, and confused. In situations like these, we tend to blame something or someone, but what do you do when that is not possible? You turn to yourself, desperately trying to map out what you did wrong and what you can do to change things for the better. It's like entering a forest you've never visited before. It's lonely at first, and you keep on moving to find your way out. You start running, to avoid missing out on anything on the other side. There are lots of branches in the way, the rain is lashing your face, and you might trip, but eventually you will reach the other side. You may exit looking and feeling a bit different—and all of a sudden you may realize that what you ran toward does not serve you anymore.

I wish that we wouldn't need to go through hardship in order to pause and evaluate our lives. The sooner we realize that we all have a choice and the power to live our lives the way we wish, the more time we'll have to enjoy them. My story is a friendly reminder that we all need a break sometimes to decide what is important.

Life Happens is fiction, and many of the characters and events are from my imagination, even though they were inspired by my own experiences.

PART 1

CHAPTER 1
Dublin, Ireland, January 2015

I was woken up by an annoying sound. It was one of those standard signals that come with the phone, and this sound got more intense by the minute. It screamed like a baby for attention, and I moaned and tried to reach for the phone on the bedside table with only minimal effort. My poor attempt to kill the sound resulted in me knocking the phone over, including the charger and my pocketbook. I sighed and got up to find the freakin' device. As soon as I found it, I pressed "Snooze" and snuck back into my warm bed. I wrapped the duvet around myself and closed my eyes. Whoever invented early-morning meetings must be evil. Wait a minute . . . morning meetings! My brain slowly came to life. Was it Tuesday today? With a blink I was wide awake and springing up. God, today was really not the day to be late!

I rushed to the shower, but my roommate had gotten there before me. I swore and went back to my room. We had recently moved in together and had not had the time to find out each other's routines yet. I caught myself wondering how many twenty-eight-year-olds shared an apartment nowadays. Sometimes I felt like I was still living the life of a student, even though I was a full-time employee at an international company in a foreign country.

I heard her singing loud and clear and couldn't help smiling. Even though it would be nice to have my own bathroom, it was definitely more fun this way.

I opened up my closet, trying to decide what to wear. All my blouses were wrinkled, and I damned the fact that I hadn't prepared these things the day before. Oh well, nothing else to do but bring out the iron and ironing board. I did a halfhearted attempt to make a blouse presentable, while glancing at my watch every other second. Shit—I could not be late! I decided that the blouse looked fine and yanked the plug from the wall. I heard the sound of a pair of naked feet patter next to me and realized Nelly was done in the shower. Her voice was worried when she said, "Anna, are you OK? It sounded like something fell!" I looked up at her. She was wrapped in a pink towel and had created a matching turban around her hair. Damn, even when she was stressed she looked good! It wasn't fair.

"Yeah, I'm fine—just overslept," I said, while heading for the bathroom. "Look, I'm really late, gonna jump in the shower." Grabbing my toothbrush, I wondered if I could shower and brush my teeth at the same time. I decided it was probably a bad idea and put the brush back on the shelf.

Twenty-five minutes later I locked the door and ran toward the garage to get my bike. While making my way through the parked cars, I prayed it wouldn't rain.

Dublin is one of those places where it rains every other day, even if only for an hour or so. Today my prayers were heard, and I arrived safe and dry at the office with a few minutes to spare. I parked the bike and hurried toward the canteen, placing my laptop on one of the tables. I was starving but realized that I wouldn't have enough time for breakfast today. Instead I rushed toward the barista. Coffee was not negotiable on a day like this! Back at the computer I opened up my email while giving the breakfast buffet a last dreaming glance. By now I had gotten used to the perks and the free food; too bad I never had time to take advantage of it, though. I had received over forty new emails since yesterday evening. Suddenly I got a burning feeling in the left side of my stomach. I sighed and put my hand over it. It had gotten worse the last couple of weeks, and I should have probably gotten it checked, but I never seemed to have the time. I was pretty sure it was stress related, even though I didn't want to admit it. I glanced at my watch and realized I needed to head for the meeting room if I was going to make it in time.

A few minutes later I opened the door to a bright room and saw that my colleague William and a man whom I assumed to be our client were already sitting down.

The client was in his early thirties and stood up to shake my hand. He introduced himself as Mr. Blake, the CEO of Fashionable.com. William and I had already been working extensively on his account with some of his employees, but I had never met him in person and was shocked by his youth. He wore a denim shirt and faded, slightly ripped jeans that matched a pair of colorful sneakers. I had expected someone in his fifties and realized he must have had a crazy career to get where he was already.

William had his best shirt on, a light-blue design from Ralph Lauren. Both the shirt and his black glasses were expensive, but he didn't look overdressed. In sneakers and jeans, he looked proper but relaxed. Other than a tic of pulling his hand through his short blond hair, he seemed to have things under control, while I tried to hide how nervous I was. I was brand new at the company, and this client was one of the biggest we had. I was terrified to get questions I couldn't answer. I had spent the whole weekend and most of the night before preparing my slides carefully so everything would be perfect. I held back a yawn and started talking about investments for the coming year. Our client gave my presentation a glance but didn't seem that interested. I felt my breath quicken and heard my manager's voice echo inside my head: "We can't afford to lose this client!"

"Listen, I want to see results, and when I do, I can invest any number you like. I just can't put the money into a black hole, though. I need to present a positive ROI." He spoke calmly and with authority. It didn't matter how much my colleague and I tried to explain the importance of brand building, even though he wouldn't get immediate sales out of it. When the discussion didn't move forward, we changed our strategy and asked what he needed at the moment. It worked much better, and Mr. Blake seemed to have lots of ideas. Before we wrapped up, he promised to share more information regarding his company's other marketing channels, and in exchange we promised our full support 24-7.

After the meeting I started to dig through my inbox, and after what felt like a thousand emails I gave up and walked over to William's desk. We went out for lunch to get some fresh air. He was in a great mood, pulling out joke after joke. I tried to keep up a good face while secretly wondering how the hell he could be so relaxed right then. I felt like all my preparations for the meeting had been in vain. I had no problem working overtime and weekends, as long as it resulted in great deals that could benefit me in my career, but this meeting felt like a huge failure and total waste of time.

William led me to a seafood restaurant close by, and we stopped outside to study the menu. Judging by the prices, the place was fancy, and I could see William's eyes light up when he saw the many awards it had received. I couldn't have cared less, and he must have noticed because he stopped reading about clams and looked at me.

"OK, what's the matter? I've never seen you this quiet."

I sighed. "I just wish the meeting had gone better, that's all."

"What do you mean? It went great! Listen, he practically promised us a yearlong commitment. He wants to work with us. That's a massive win!"

"Yeah, but I kind of hoped we would close a deal then and there. I'm sorry, but unless the papers are signed, I can't jump for joy."

"Well, you should, because these things take time. What matters is that we have established a relationship, and that's huge. Now we have something to build on."

"It's just that . . . I put so much work into the presentation and he barely looked at it."

"Look, that happens. It was good that you brought it—it showed that we were serious."

"If you say so." I followed him inside, even though I had lost my appetite.

"Chin up, I have a feeling this will be huge. You just wait."

I heard what he was saying but couldn't absorb it. I was all for being positive, but this time I felt like we had no reason to be.

***

Later that evening, a random slam from a nearby door woke me up briskly. I yawned and checked my watch. It showed almost ten in the evening, and I looked around. I was the only one left, except for the cleaning staff, and the lights had just started to go out, meaning that I would now have to move my arms above my head like a crazy person every tenth minute to activate the motion sensors. I was sure those lights were great for the environment, but they were incredibly annoying. I looked at my to-do list, and I was still not even close to being done. I rubbed my eyes and went to grab an apple.

When I sat down by the computer again, I closed my eyes and whispered to myself, "I love my job. I have chosen this. I love my job." I couldn't help but wonder how everyone else on my team managed to leave work on time. To make things easier, I imagined myself at a homecoming event that would happen sooner or later at my former university. It was that moment when old classmates meet and put on a great big smile. Nobody says it out loud, but everybody is aware that it's a competition. They ask where you live, where you work, what position you have at the company, while secretly judging and trying to find out if you have a more promising career than they do. I leaned back in my chair and imagined their admiring faces when I told them that I worked for *the* company in the tech business. The company that topped the list of most desirable employers several years in a row. Even so, I felt I wasn't good enough. Sometimes I got a feeling that it had been a mistake that I'd gotten this position, and I was just waiting for the day when they would find out. I guessed that was one of the reasons I worked such long hours. To prove them wrong, but also to prove it to myself. My logical side told me the thorough interview process I'd gone through before receiving an offer should have given them a pretty good picture of my abilities. But that was my logical side. My self-esteem was not as easily convinced.

CHAPTER 2

The next day I was dead tired. I guess the long hours of work were starting to catch up with me. I stood at my adjustable standing desk, massaging my temples, when a reminder popped up on my screen. We had a team meeting in five minutes. I sighed deeply and reached for the small heart-shaped toy next to the keyboard. It was soft and squishy; pressing it was supposed to relieve stress. I squeezed it hard. These meetings took almost an hour, and all we did was confirm that we were behind our targets. If everyone just left me alone and let me do my job instead of having so many meetings, we wouldn't be behind. I thought I would use the last minutes to finish up an email when a senior colleague stopped by.

"Hey, what's up? You look focused."

I started chewing on my lower lip. Whenever he came over I knew I wouldn't get anything done. He never stopped talking. I gave up and turned away from my desk, still with an eye on the email. When I looked at him I couldn't help taking a step back to be able to see his face properly. I always forgot how tall he was. Next to him I felt like a midget, even though I was pretty tall myself. "Just trying to finish up before the meeting, that's all. How are you?"

"Good, good. Or, it was good till a minute ago, when I looked at our numbers. To be honest, it doesn't look that bright. End of quarter is closing in."

The pain in my stomach called for attention again, but I forced myself to keep calm and gave him a forced smile. I wanted to scream that I was already working like an animal, and that I wished he would go away. I didn't need him to tell me the obvious, but he didn't seem to get the hint.

"Yep, I guess it's gonna be a few hectic weeks ahead," he said.

"I know. I'm working as fast as I can."

"Might be time to work faster." He laughed at his own joke and thumped me hard on the back. His palms were huge, and he didn't seem aware that his touch almost made me lose my breath. "Hey, maybe we should get going?" He started to walk toward the conference room. When he noticed I hadn't joined him, he turned around. "You coming?"

"Yeah. I just need a minute in the ladies' room. You go ahead."

I never joined that meeting. I felt the tears burning in the corner of my eyes, and I rushed to the bathroom. My plan was to pour some cold water on my face to calm down, and I thought maybe I could be a few minutes late. Unfortunately I wasn't alone. Jasmine, another coworker, was standing by the mirrors opposite the toilet stalls, applying some lipstick. Before I could escape, she saw me and turned around. "Whoa, slow down, missy." When she saw my tense expression, she fastened her eyes on mine. "Are you OK?"

All it took was a small act of kindness, and tears started pouring down my face.

"I just don't know how I'm gonna make it this quarter," I whispered between the tears. "I'm behind targets."

"Girl, is that it? Everybody is behind! They set them so high to make us work harder. In the end we always make it."

"Yeah, but I don't know . . . maybe I'm not good enough." A sudden fear crept up on me, and I got cold. "Oh God, what if they fire me?"

"You need to stop." Her voice got firmer, and she removed a black strand of hair from her face. "Of course they wouldn't. I've seen your work; you are great. It's our targets that are fucked up. You need to have more faith in yourself."

She turned away to get some paper towels for me to dry my tears.

"I need to go to the meeting," she said. "Will you be OK? If you don't want to go, I can make up an excuse for you."

I smiled through the tears. "Thanks—you're the best. I'm just gonna calm down; I'll be out later."

"Of course, take your time." She started to walk toward the door, then hesitated and turned around. "Hey, what are you doing tonight?"

I wiped away another tear. "Eh, working, I guess."

"No, missy, you're not. Come to my place and have some tea. You need a break. Around eight p.m.?" It wasn't an invite—it was more like an order.

I gave in. I knew I wouldn't be able to be so productive after this little breakdown anyway. I nodded slowly. "I'll be there." She gave me a broad smile that showed her perfect teeth.

"OK, see you later then. I'll text you the address."

After she disappeared, I went inside one of the stalls to have some privacy. I leaned my head against the door and tried to breathe deeply. What had happened? I knew I could be emotional, but this? In the middle of a working day? I hoped I wasn't going to lose it completely. I thought about it and concluded that my reaction must have been a mix of stress and lack of sleep. And then such a small thing as the comment from my colleague had been the last straw. It was typical me, though, to think that he'd referred only to *my* work when he said that "we" needed to work faster. I repeated to myself, "Everybody is behind, it's not just me. It's not just me." I took another deep breath before I went out to the sink by the mirrors, splashed some water on my face, and returned to my desk. I could still get things done today.

***

Later that evening I rang the doorbell of Jasmine's flat. She opened it, and I couldn't help but smile. She had a huge pink sweater on that was almost like a dress on her petite figure. Her name suited her, as she looked like the character from *Aladdin*, with her dark hair that waved naturally. She had big brown eyes, and her skin tone was slightly darker than my pale appearance. I was jealous—it was like she had a naturally soft tan year-round. "Come in, come in. I've put on the tea. I have this nice detox tea you need to try. It tastes just like green apple!" She spun around the kitchen and brought out cups and some chocolate treats. I looked around for somewhere to sit and decided that the sofa was the best place. She had a nice home—the ceiling was high, and it felt spacious, even though it was just an average apartment for one. The kitchen was more like a small pantry, and there was no wall separating it from the living room. She had decorated her sofa with cushions in different warm colors. Each cushion had small sequins that outlined different patterns like flowers and elephants. On the table in front of me were candles that gave a soothing light, and incense that made the room smell like vanilla. It was not my style but made me feel very cozy. I pulled my feet up and reached out my hands when she came closer, balancing a tray of tea and snacks.

"You've got to try these, I made them myself." She pointed at something that looked almost like chocolate balls. "They're made purely out of dates and cashew nuts, so totally guilt free."

I reached for one and looked at it suspiciously before I took a bite. "Mm, they're good. So sweet!"

"I know, I'm kind of addicted." She smiled and took one herself.

I felt a bit awkward, as this was the first time I had been to a colleague's house. During my first week at work, Jasmine had shown me around, but then we didn't have the time to get to know each other properly. I had a hard time relaxing at work and being my normal sociable self, since I always had deadlines hanging over my shoulder. Jasmine always seemed to be in a good mood, though, friendly and willing to help.

"Listen, thanks for inviting me. I'm not proud of the incident this afternoon, as normally I'm more put together. It's just been a lot lately."

"Oh, don't worry about it. You should have seen me when I was new—I was totally freaking out. You just have to learn not to take it personally. After all, it's just work."

It felt good to hear her say that, even though I disagreed a bit. What did she mean by "just work"? For me, my career was everything, and I didn't want to fail at this opportunity. I guess I just had to learn how to handle the pressure. How I would do so was a different question.

It was like she had read my mind. "Hey, I used to be just like you. I worked long hours, I was ambitious, wanted to do a good job. But you have to realize that it's not worth it in the long run. If you reach your targets, you might get a pat on the back, but then you'll have higher targets the next quarter. It never ends, and remember, nobody will thank you if you get burned out—they will just hire someone else. I know it sounds harsh, but we are replaceable."

I took a sip of my tea and tried to take in what she had just said. It went against everything I believed. "I think I put my work before my health," I said slowly. "I always have."

"Why?" Her question was sharp, and I almost got annoyed. Wasn't it obvious?

"Well, I'm convinced that if I just work hard enough, I'll get my dream job. When I was younger, I decided that if I had to spend a lot of time on something, I might as well enjoy what I'm doing."

"And are you?"

I let the question hang in the air for a moment while trying to determine her intentions. Her big eyes seemed kind, and her voice was soft. She wasn't there to put me in my place; she seemed genuinely interested in my well-being.

"I guess so . . . if I could take away the stress, it's actually fun."

"So don't let it get to you! Leave when I leave in the evenings, don't work so hard."

It sounded so easy, but I couldn't help but wonder if she would get promoted with that mind-set.

"Let's talk about something more fun!" she said and put her hands together. "Seen any cute guys lately?"

Her question took me back a little. Of course, there were a lot of cute guys at work, but I hadn't really dated much. I didn't want to admit it, but I still had a thing for Carl, a guy from Sweden.

"Well . . . my love life stands pretty still at the moment," I said, shrugging my shoulders.

"Sweetie, that can be changed." Her eyes sparkled as if she were up to something. Jasmine reached for her phone and showed me a dating app she used. Soon we were busy searching for the perfect match, giggling like girls.

As I biked home that evening, my heart felt lighter. I'd needed that break, even though I felt a sting of guilt that I had taken the evening off. I knew it would bite me in the ass the next day, but I convinced myself it was worth it.

CHAPTER 3

The days flew by, and I kept on working hard, even though I tried to take into account what Jasmine had said. I still worked long hours, but I tried to take breaks to go to the gym. It made me tired, but I forced myself to keep going. After all, it was supposed to give more energy than it consumed, right?

I had constant guilt over not having enough time for exercise, so when a guy approached me in the gym and asked if I would be up for running every now and then, I said yes. He was in way better shape than me, but I didn't mind, as I needed someone to push me. Our schedules were different, and we decided to go running during lunch instead of after work. The day of our first scheduled run, at noon when everybody else headed to the canteen, I grabbed my workout bag and shut down my computer. I quickly changed into workout gear and had a sip of water before heading toward the reception area to meet him.

"Hey! Right on time," he said, smiling and holding open the door.

I laughed. "Well, I guess I'm Swedish after all." He was a bit taller than me and looked like he had been taken straight from a health magazine. I didn't know anybody who could claim to be more fit than he was. I remembered the heavy weights he had been lifting in the gym, and I hoped I had not taken on more than I could manage. He had short blond hair, and his accent gave away that he came from a German-speaking country.

We didn't spend time warming up; instead, we started running toward the beach straightaway while talking about small stuff. I learned that he traveled a lot: almost every second weekend he went somewhere to go surfing or skiing. He told me he had been in the military and ran marathons every now and then. I swallowed. All of a sudden my 10K once a week didn't seem that impressive. I just prayed I could keep up with him without completely embarrassing myself.

After about forty-five minutes of running, my legs felt heavy and I got afraid they would give in at any moment. I warned him that I might have to stop soon. Then he told me that soldiers in the military would sometimes press gently on one another's backs to keep themselves running. Now he was doing the same to me, and I wanted to punch him, but somehow I kept on moving until we reached the office. My face was burning, and I wouldn't have been surprised if it was dark red, as I was completely out of breath. I leaned forward and held my hands on my knees to prevent them from shaking. I looked up at him through my sweaty fringe. "You know, you really killed me out there."

He laughed and ran his hands through his hair. "That's good, though, that's the only way to get better," he said with a friendly smile. He started jumping on the spot so as not to get cold. He didn't look half as tired as I felt, and he reminded me of a puppy that had just gotten in from a long walk and was ready to go for another one straightaway.

"Same time next week?" He started stretching his calves.

I wanted to tell him that I would never do that again, that he was mad to work out this hard, and that I had better things to do, but then my pride and competitiveness took over. "Yeah, sure."

We went into the office together and made a high five before going into separate dressing rooms. Once the door closed behind me, I took a deep breath and staggered along toward the showers. I had to use the wall to help me sit down on a bench. For a while I just sat there, leaning my head against the lockers. Closing my eyes, I could feel the endorphins starting to flood through my system. I was completely exhausted but happy that I'd managed to push myself to a new level. Too bad there was no time for a nap now. I leaned back and tried to prepare myself mentally to shower, grab a quick lunch, and return to the computer.

***

Back at my desk, I went through my to-do list to decide how to structure the rest of the day. As usual, I had a guilty conscience for exercising instead of working, but I tried to tell myself that it would make me healthier and more efficient in the long run. I didn't feel the benefits at the moment, though, that was for sure. My legs were like jelly, and I had to adjust my stand-up desk and pull out a chair. No way I was going to manage to stand at the computer today. It was already one thirty, which got me a bit stressed, since I had promised a client a presentation the next morning. *Oh well, I can always stay late*, I thought, and I glanced at my calendar. *Wait, were Nelly's birthday drinks tonight? Damn, how would I manage to attend and still get all this work done?* There was no way I could miss it, as that would make me a lousy friend, and it was important that I attended these events for networking purposes. The pain in the side of my stomach started to creep up on me, screaming for attention. I placed my hand over it and pressed gently, as sometimes that helped. I knew by now it had to be stress related, and I cursed the fact that I couldn't handle my life better. Everyone else seemed to be so calm and to have their lives in order. It seemed like they could balance work and private life with no big effort, and here I was feeling like I was failing. Something started to vibrate in my pocket, and I almost jumped. Pulling up my phone, I saw that the screen showed a text from Nelly saying *"Can't wait for tonight—let's go all in!"* Oh my God, I knew what that meant. The birthday drinks would turn into a full night of clubbing. Normally I loved to go crazy, and when I was a student it had been no problem. You just made sure you didn't have an early lecture the next day, and even if you did, nothing would happen if you showed up late. Nowadays it was different. Being hungover at work didn't go hand in hand with reaching targets. Leaning back on my chair, I gave a tired smile. I guess this was a dilemma for those in the spoiled, developed nations. After all, it was only fun stuff we were talking about. I just had to get a grip, grab an extra coffee, and get through it.

***

That evening I lasted till midnight before I felt I couldn't continue even if somebody forced me. I needed rest, so I took a taxi home while my friends were still dancing up a storm at the club. Maybe I would have done the same if it had been my birthday, but it was the middle of the week and my body was screaming for sleep. I felt like I'd just wasted my workout from earlier that day by having drink after drink. Damn it, I couldn't seem to get anything right. How did everybody else do it?

I was awoken by the taxi driver shaking my shoulder. "Miss, here we are." I blinked drowsily, still half asleep, and realized he was right. I could see my apartment complex through the window and felt my cheeks turn red in embarrassment. I apologized while reaching for my wallet. *I really need to get a grip*, I said to myself while slowly making my way toward the entrance. I knew somewhere in the back of my head that I needed to slow things down, but I easily got caught up in my surroundings and didn't know how to say no. After all, I wanted all of this, didn't I?

I spent a good ten minutes trying to find the keys in my bag, and in my drunken state everything seemed like a challenge. When I finally found them and stumbled inside, I didn't even bother taking my clothes off before passing out on the bed.

CHAPTER 4

A sharp, buzzing sound reminded me it was morning, and I sent a thankful thought to Nelly for setting my alarm the night before. My throat was dry, and my tongue felt like it had grown to twice its size. I knew a headache was creeping up on me, no matter how much I wished it wouldn't. It took a few minutes of massaging my temples and groaning in self-pity before I forced myself to sit up. I had to hold my head in my hands for a moment to block out the sunshine that was percolating through the window. There was only one thought in my head, and that was to get water. Dragging myself to the kitchen I emptied two full glasses before heading for the shower. A few minutes later I hit my toes while trying to find something to wear. I swore out loud and jumped on one foot till the pain went away. I clenched my teeth and breathed heavily through my nose. This would be a long day.

***

It was Wednesday, when I had my regular coaching meeting with my manager. A few minutes before it was to start, I sat in a small conference room with bright green walls. It was empty except for a table and six chairs in different colors. I was pretty happy that it was just going to be the two of us, since I needed all the air I could get that day. I had taken some acetaminophen but was still not feeling well. The lamps were bright to make up for the fact that there were no windows. My manager came one minute late, and he had to catch his breath before we started. While he was busy starting his laptop, I couldn't help but notice that his shirt seemed looser than usual. Had he lost some weight? He usually went from meeting to meeting, never allowing himself a break. I guess stress affected us all differently. He ran his hands through his thinning hair and started talking about goals. It seemed crucial to him, and it didn't take long before he asked if I had a five-year career plan. He asked if I felt stressed and told me how important it was for him that I felt I had his support, no matter what.

I tried to put up a good face—after all, nobody likes a fragile player. I wanted to tell him I felt overwhelmed by the amount of work, and that I didn't know how much longer I could take it. Instead, I put on my game face and said that everything was fine, that I planned on staying in the company, aiming for a promotion. Technically, it wasn't a lie. I mean, I knew I didn't have the work–life balance that was preached as so important, but it was true that I was aiming to climb the career ladder, and I couldn't see how that would happen without lots of work.

"Well, just keep doing what you're doing and you'll be fine," he said vaguely. He tapped his fingers on the table and seemed keen to move on. "I know you have a few projects on the side, but there is actually something I need your help with."

My eyes grew wide. *No, please no, don't ask me for anything more right now.*

I leaned forward with my palms on my knees to show my interest—and at the same time to hide my shaking hands.

"I need someone to take care of this new project promoting us as an employer in the Nordic countries. It will mean more traveling for you, but I will allocate five percent of your time for it. Since you have been arranging events and such before, I believe you would be perfect."

Oh great, one of those projects that require a lot of work while preventing you from doing your core job. I couldn't say I was thrilled. I knew about this position, but I had purposely not applied since I could barely handle my primary responsibilities at the moment. Now my manager sat in front of me asking me to do it, and there was nowhere to hide.

"I don't know—" I started but was interrupted by him.

"Anna, I would really appreciate if you did this."

Oh shit, he was playing that card. I was still in the beginning of my career and had no idea how the internal politics worked, but I did know that if your manager specifically asked you for something, you didn't say no.

My spare time disappeared before my eyes as I swallowed hard and said, "Of course—if you need me to do it, I will."

I was tired. I knew how hard I had to work to even get considered for promotion, and if this was what it was going to take, I had to prioritize it. It was probably for the best, and it was what I wanted, right? I decided to stop feeling sorry for myself. I didn't put in all those hours of studying in high school and later at university to give up now because I was a bit worn out. Now wasn't the time to start taking it easy.

"Great. I will forward an email with all the details." He looked relieved and put his hands together. "So, if there is nothing else you want to bring up, I think we are done."

We stood up and left the room together. On the way back to our desks, I couldn't help but wonder if he had asked me because I was the best person for the job or because he'd known I wouldn't say no. My pocket started to vibrate. It was Nelly, who admitted she felt like shit because of the night before. She suggested leaving the office early for dinner. I can't say I wasn't tempted. I hesitated a few minutes, then I wrote her back that it was hectic at work and that I had to stay late. She texted right back, saying that I was quite a bore and that I should tell her when I changed my mind. I promised I would, even though I knew right then that I wouldn't make it, not with this new project going on.

CHAPTER 5

That weekend Nelly and I decided to go to Ikea. I had mixed feelings about it. I knew that it wouldn't be any fun shopping, because we needed only boring things for our home, like cutting boards, a frying pan, cleaning supplies, and God knows what else. I'd rather have used my money for a new pair of shoes, but I knew we had to do this. Becoming a grown-up wasn't always fun. On the other hand, Ikea always made me a bit nostalgic, in a good way. After all, it was a piece of home, and I smiled when I thought of it. It was kind of ironic: when I was in Sweden, I didn't care, but the moment I set my foot abroad, I started clinging to my traditions. Even Kalles Kaviar, a popular caviar in a tube that I normally wouldn't eat, seemed tempting when I knew the supply was limited.

Saturday morning, I heated water and prepared my french press. Now this was the best investment I had made so far! I wondered how bad it was that I drank so much coffee every day. I could go without breakfast and miss out on some sleep, but if I didn't get my coffee in the morning, I argued that I couldn't be held responsible for the consequences. It was a less likeable side of me, but when I thought of the other addictions out there, I decided it couldn't be so bad. As I stirred the black powder into the glass carafe, I started to feel a bit dizzy. At first I didn't pay attention to it; after all, it was morning and I hadn't had breakfast yet. I pulled the yogurt from the fridge and reached for the muesli on the counter next to it. As I headed for the fruit bowl, I started to see tiny black spots in front of my eyes. It was the same feeling you get when you rise too fast after sitting or lying down. *Maybe I should take it slower*, I thought, as sometimes my blood pressure was low. I blinked to make the spots go away, but they didn't disappear; instead, they intensified. It was like a group of fireflies were flying in front of my eyes, but instead of bright yellow, they were all black. I closed my eyes for a few seconds, but when I opened them, the spots were still there. I made my way to the kitchen table, pulled out a chair, and sat down. Now this was weird. Nelly came into the kitchen. She was already dressed.

"Morning!" Her voice was light and bubbly, and I could tell she'd had a good night's sleep. "I'm so looking forward to Ikea. I'm gonna try to find a new wardrobe for my room. And maybe some more stuff, you know how it goes." She was looking through the fridge for something to eat and pulled out what I thought were berries, but I couldn't make out what kind from where I was sitting. "You want me to bring you your stuff? It's still here on the counter." She turned around and stopped in the middle of a step. "You OK?" I had put my head between my knees in a poor attempt to get some more blood flowing through my brain.

I sat up properly. "This might sound weird, but I can barely see you."

She put what I thought was my bowl of yogurt on the table, and I could feel her penetrating look. "What do you mean?"

"Well, I think I rose too fast this morning, and I started to see spots in front of my eyes. Could be my low blood pressure.

But now . . . there are so many I can't see properly. They won't go away."

I heard her pull out the chair next to me. "Whoa, don't scare me like that. You probably just need to rest. Did you have coffee?"

I slowly shook my head. I could hear her getting up, and when she returned, the familiar dark-roasted scent filled my nostrils. I could hear the sound of china when she put down the cup in front of me on the glass table.

"Here, some coffee will help you get going."

I turned to her and couldn't help laughing at the situation. "This is so weird, I really can't see you."

I heard her move around on her chair. "That *is* weird. I think you should rest. We can leave a bit later, if you want."

"No, I think I'll be fine. I'm just gonna sit here for a moment." I saw a shadow that I assumed was my cup and reached for it. I took a sip and closed my eyes.

***

Two hours later we pulled up in the parking lot of the big warehouse. We grabbed one shopping cart each and steered toward the entrance. My eyesight was back, and I had shrugged off the unpleasant start of the day.

I wanted to go straight to the kitchen supplies, but a glance on the orientation map reminded me that Ikea doesn't work like that. "You need to go through all the sections before you reach the exit?" Nelly asked. She looked over my shoulder and started tapping her foot.

I nodded. "Well, since this is your first time here, you might as well see it all. They have a café too."

"Yay!" She ran off like a kid in a candy store, and I smiled broadly a few minutes later when I saw her excitement over a pink flamingo lamp. I couldn't help but think of how well thought out this store was from a merchandise perspective. You walked through different rooms that displayed all the items and made it look homey. All the inspiration you needed was there. Even someone with no interest in home décor would start thinking of redecorating. Nelly had already put quite a few things in her basket, and I had a hard time keeping up with her pace.

They must be big on complementary selling, I thought with a look at the bathroom section. Next to the towels, the matching bathroom carpets were displayed. There were funky toothbrush holders that you didn't need but that went well with the new carpet. Or, wait, did you really buy that, too? It was brilliant, and I could easily see how Ikea made its millions.

We had now reached the bedroom section, and I was just about to head for the pillowcases when I bumped into a lady. She turned around with an annoyed wrinkle between her eyes. Her voice was sharp, and her curly red hair jumped up and down as she half screamed, "Look where you're going, will ya! God, I hope I didn't sprain my ankle." I apologized several times and made sure she calmed down before I continued my shopping journey. I couldn't help feeling a bit confused . . . Where had she come from? I hadn't been walking fast, and I swear I hadn't seen her coming. I thought about it some more and grimaced—maybe she was the one who had bumped into me. Anyway, I saw that Nelly was way ahead and steered my cart toward her.

Somewhere between the section for carpets and paintings, I felt like all my blood rushed to my toes, and I had to get a firmer grip around the handle of the shopping cart. I stopped for a moment. The spots were back. Was this a freakin' joke? What was going on? Feeling weak, I realized that lying down would probably be a good idea. I turned the cart around and headed back to the beds and pillows. I found a bed in a corner and parked my cart next to it. I sat down and took a deep breath, then leaned myself back and closed my eyes. This must have looked so weird, and I hoped I wouldn't see anyone I knew.

I don't know how long I laid there, but it was well over half an hour. I'd just wanted to make my head stop spinning, and I wondered if I'd boosted Ikea's sales by showcasing how comfortable the bed was. *They should pay me*, I thought with a weak smile.

"There you are! I've been looking all over for you. Why aren't you answering your phone?" Nelly paused and removed some blond hair from her eyes. "What is with you?" Nelly looked down at me with her big blue eyes, her hands on her waist. "You are starting to freak me out."

I blinked and held up one hand to protect me from the bright light. "To be honest, I don't feel that well."

"I can see that." Her eyebrows were now drawn together and her voice got softer. "Do you need anything? Water?"

"No, I'm fine," I said and pulled myself up to a sitting position. "I think I will just wait here while you finish your shopping, if that's OK. I don't know what's happening. I'm not myself today. Maybe I can't handle alcohol anymore." I winked at her. The night before had been quite rough on both of us. We had gone out clubbing with some friends, and I'd known I shouldn't have had that last drink. Was I getting old?

She hesitated. "I don't wanna leave you here. Are you sure you are OK?"

"Yes, yes—I just need to take it easy. You go ahead. If I feel better, I will catch up."

***

I didn't catch up with her. In fact, I felt worse and started to suspect I had caught a cold of some sort. We met up about an hour later by the cashiers, and I was impressed by her shopping speed. When I'd gone to Ikea with my parents as a kid, we always spent the whole day. Nelly pulled out her phone from her pocket, and we took several selfies. She chose the best one and let our smiling faces start to gather likes on Facebook before we headed for the parking lot. I felt a bit embarrassed to put up such a charade. Most of our friends would spend the day in the bathroom or in bed, waiting for the alcohol to leave their bodies. And here we were, screaming for attention. "Look at us, best roomies spend quality time together while improving our new apartment... while you guys are wasting your day." Of course we didn't write that, but it was the underlying message. How easy it was to create an illusion that was quite far from the truth. On the way home I tried to look straight ahead, focusing on the road so as not to get nauseated. I couldn't wait to get into my bed. Once we got home, I changed to pajamas and parked myself with my laptop in bed, even though it was only around six. I thought it must be a weird type of hangover and decided that Netflix could fix it.

CHAPTER 6

The next day I had new energy, and the worries from the day before faded away quickly. I thanked my lucky stars and was in a great mood as I walked into the office. My meetings went smoothly, and by lunchtime I was on top of my game, satisfied that I had been so productive. The conference I initiated was approved, and my excitement was mixed with fear. If I made sure it was successful, it would look great in front of my manager. It would also be time-consuming, and I was already struggling to get everything done. Oh well—I didn't have time to think about that now. A new email popped up on my screen, and I had to get closer to see what it said. I scratched my eyes and wondered if it was time to change the monthly contacts already.

"Hungry?" I jumped at the sudden voice. Jasmine was standing close by to my left, and I thought it was strange that I hadn't seen her coming.

"Everything all right?" she asked with a humorous twinkle in her eyes, clearly amused by my reaction.

"Yeah, I was just in my own world. You scared me a little."

"Oh, I'm sorry!" She gave me a hug, and I tried not to squeeze her fragile body too much. I smiled when she didn't let go at first and remembered her saying something way back about the perfect hug. Apparently it should last seven seconds, to nurture our souls and make us feel loved. It sounded like something somebody had made up, but I believed it worked, and I instantly felt more relaxed and decided the email could wait.

Twenty minutes later we sat on the thirteenth floor with a salad each, enjoying the view through the tall windows reaching from the ceiling to the floor. From there you could see all the way to Sandymount, one of the many areas of Dublin. We could see beyond the tall industrial buildings and all the way to the beach. Only one person was walking next to the glittering water, and his dog was stirring up a group of seagulls while jumping around. It was such a weird mix, really: on the one hand, a peaceful scene of nature, but on the other hand, the dark smoke pouring from the chimneys in the distance. It had been raining, but now the sun was starting to come out. A few sunbeams were already sneaking through the gray clouds and creating a warm and hopeful yellow light. Even though it would have been nicer without the factories, the scene was somehow beautiful. We were talking about the weekend. Jasmine had been to yoga both days and was trying to convince me to try it. "It's the absolute best way to start a day," she said with genuine enthusiasm. "You ease into the day and start it completely stress-free."

"I don't know . . . I believe I'm too restless. I'm more the running kinda girl," I said, and we left the topic.

I told her about the incident at Ikea. Her big brown eyes studied me without blinking, and her otherwise smooth forehead became wrinkled. *Shit, I knew I shouldn't have told her.*

"Anna," she said resolutely, "you should go and get it checked."

"Yeah, I know." I looked out the windows. "But I don't have the time right now."

"Of course you do! That's why we have a doctor right here at the office. You don't have any excuse, just give them a call—or stop by their reception. It'll take you a few minutes."

She grasped my arm and gave me a stern look. She didn't look away until I started to laugh. "OK, OK—I'll call them straightaway after this."

"Good." She leaned back on her chair in ease and relaxed her shoulders. "Nothing is more important than your health. You need to remember that."

I regretted I'd even brought it up; now I had to call the doctor. I knew Jasmine would ask me later. We finished our meals and headed back to our floor. I spent a few minutes just looking at the phone before I dialed the number. The receptionist told me they'd had a cancellation and that I could have an appointment an hour later. I thanked her and continued working. The doctor's office was in the same building, and it would take me only a few minutes to get there.

**

The doctor was running late. I sat in the waiting room and browsed through a magazine about women's health. I looked at my watch. *If I had known this, I would have brought my computer*, I thought, a bit annoyed. Ten more minutes passed before the door opened and the doctor called my name. I sat down in the visitor's chair and looked around while she pulled up my file on the computer. It was quite a small room—I would guess about 100 square feet. Except for her desk, the examination bed, and a shelf, there was no other furniture. A big poster of a furry white cat lit up the room and made it less sterile.

The doctor introduced herself as Dr. Grady. She had dark brown hair cut in a neat page, and I guessed she was in her fifties. Something about her made me calm. Maybe it was her tidy appearance, with a cardigan in pink pastel and discreet jewelry, or the perfect piles of paper on her desk. She seemed orderly, just as you'd expect a doctor to be.

"What can I help you with today?"

I was a bit embarrassed and looked down. By now I was convinced it could not be anything other than my blood pressure, and I felt bad for wasting her time.

I told her about the Ikea incident and mentioned that my sight had gotten bad on my left side. She asked what I meant, and I described the feeling I'd had when Jasmine approached me before lunch. I hadn't seen her coming at all until she was right next to me. I remembered the stomachache and figured it couldn't hurt to tell her about that, too. She took my blood pressure and confirmed it was normal. After some more-detailed questions, she confirmed that the stomach pain was caused by stress, and the issue with the vision was probably nothing. Her advice was to take it easier and drink plenty of water. I thanked her for her time and got up. Great, almost half an hour wasted. I bumped into the doorframe on my way out and tried to look unconcerned while heading for the receptionist to pay. How embarrassing! I hoped nobody had seen anything.

As I was about to enter my PIN, the door opened behind me and Dr. Grady called me back. She said she just wanted to check one more thing, as after all, not everyone walks straight into doorframes in the middle of the day. She did a simple visual field test in which she held out her arms and slowly moved them toward the middle where I sat. I was asked to keep my eyes focused on her nose and to let her know when I saw her hands clearly. After she was done, she became silent, and the only noise that could be heard was her scratching her hair. It got all messed up and destroyed her clean look.

"Listen . . ." she said slowly and bit her lip. "You are right; it seems like your visual field is not perfect. I am not sure why, since you haven't had any problems in the past. I think it's important we get it checked, though, so I'm going to send you to a specialist, OK?"

I sighed. "Are you sure that is necessary?" I felt the minutes disappear before my eyes. If I had to go to another doctor, I would probably not get anything more done that day.

She leaned forward. "I believe it's important. After all, your health is the most important thing you have."

Oh God, not her, too. What was with everybody and health today? I promised her I would have it done that day and headed for my desk to get my jacket.

***

A few hours later I was sitting in a waiting room on the other end of town with about thirty other people. It seemed like this was the only place for eye issues, and apparently I had picked the wrong day. I glanced at my watch. Five p.m. I texted Jasmine: "*This takes ages. Will probably not come back to the office today, will work from home. Can you tell our manager?*" I leaned back and sighed. Was this really necessary? I looked around and saw a small boy with a cotton pad taped above his left eye. A lady who I assumed was his mom held her arm around him and whispered something in his ear. He smiled. The woman to my right looked to be around sixty, and when she turned to me to ask for the time, I could see that one of her eyes was completely red. I ran my hands through my hair and rubbed the back of my head. This was silly; it seemed like these people actually had real problems. *Maybe I should leave and come back another day. I could still get a lot of work done today*, I thought. It was probably nothing, and I would just take up the doctor's precious time. I decided that was for the best and was standing up when my phone beeped. It was a text from Jasmine.

"*Good that you are looking into it!!! Promise me you will not go home until they give you an explanation. Lots of love.*"

Oh Lord, now I had no choice but to stay. I sighed deeply and sank down into my chair again.

***

My stomach was starting to rumble, and I looked at my watch. Nine p.m., and still loads of people in the waiting room but no sign of the doctor. I went over and put some change into the vending machine. I realized my dinner would consist of peanuts and chocolate. I didn't dare leave and try to find a store—they might call my name. I hadn't spent the whole afternoon there to miss my turn. My stubbornness woke to life, and I prepared myself mentally to stay the whole night if necessary.

When it was almost eleven p.m., a nurse finally called my name. She showed me into a small room, placed me in front of a machine, and gave me a little white device. The nurse told me to look straight ahead and press a button every time I could see a spot of light in the corners of my eyes. It didn't take long. She then put a liquid in my eyes that made my vision blurry. She sent me back to the waiting room and told me the doctor would see me shortly. I took a deep breath and wondered what "shortly" meant to her.

An hour later the nurse showed me into a room that didn't look like a normal office. It was quite dark, and it seemed like a room used only because of a lack of space elsewhere. Two doctors sat at desks, both busy talking to patients, and I was advised to stay in the corner and wait my turn. They were not big on privacy there, as there was not even a drapery between the tables. I sat down on a bed at the side of the room and waited. When the doctor approached me, I found myself wishing that they hadn't given me those eye drops. He was tall, young, and, from what I could tell in my blurry state, really cute. He could have replaced one of the stars in *Grey's Anatomy* any day. He asked me a few questions and then ordered me to lie down on the bed and keep still.

"Yes, please!" I wanted to shout, but instead I nodded and did what I was told. I wondered if he was single. He shone a bright light into both of my eyes, and then he used something to move my eyeballs to the side so he could get a better look. The instrument was cold, and the situation was extremely uncomfortable. I was scared he would slip and hurt my eye . . . All it would have taken was a sneeze to make him lose his balance. Could I sue him if he did? My thoughts were all over the place, but I tried to focus on keeping my head still. After what felt like an eternity, he stopped and asked me to have a seat at the desk. He sat down and looked at his computer for a couple of minutes before turning back to me with serious eyes. "Well, Ms. Larsson, I have good and bad news." It sounded like dialogue from a movie. Could he spit it out already? He made me nervous.

"So, I had a look at your visual field test, and you were right, your vision is far from perfect. You never had any problems before, you said?"

I shook my head.

"Well, it's your visual field in both eyes, but you seem to notice it more on the left. The good thing is that my examination shows no sign that there is anything wrong with your eyes. They are perfectly healthy. The bad news . . ." He hesitated, and I wished he would stop wiggling in his chair. He cleared his throat and continued, "The bad news is that it must be your head."

"Wait, what? Do I come off as that stupid?" I tried to pull off a joke, but he didn't seem amused. I tried to look unconcerned, but on the inside I was panicking. It felt like my blood slowly froze, and I couldn't have moved even if I wanted to. The doctor went on: "It could be a small stroke, and I would like you to have an MRI. Before that, we can't say anything."

I felt like fainting. A stroke? I was young and healthy—it wasn't possible! Thousands of thoughts went through my mind, but I said nothing.

"I'm sorry," he said and started to write something on his computer. "Listen, take this number." He handed me a small Post-it note. "They will call you in the next couple of days to schedule the MRI. If not, it's important that you call them."

I slowly walked out of the room and did my best not to look at the other patients who were still waiting for their turn. I didn't want anyone to see I was about to cry. In the taxi on my way home, I was upset and felt the panic rise again, but I decided to handle it like I usually did: by pretending it was nothing. Before I had any results, it wasn't worth my worry, was it?

CHAPTER 7

Three weeks later I sat in front of the same doctor again. Without the eye drops, I could finally see him clearly, and I had been right: he *was* cute. This time it was me who wiggled on the chair and looked down. I didn't want to hear what he had to say, but at the same time, I did. The past weeks had been torture. First I had to wait to get the MRI appointment, and when it was done, the results had to be sent off to be analyzed.

The doctor seemed so young, and I wondered how much experience he had. His nervous way of flipping through his papers made me uncomfortable, and I hoped he knew what he was doing.

"How have you been?" he said and gave me a quick glance.

"Good, and you?" I kept it short. In any other situation, I would have loved to have a chat with this guy, but not today. The underlying stress of not knowing what was going on, and the back-and-forth visits to different hospitals had taken their toll, and I just wanted this to be over and done with.

"Good." He swallowed and started to flip through his notes again, like he was trying to buy time. The seconds passed slowly before he finally put down the papers and looked me in the eyes. "We have looked at the scans from your MRI, and we found a shadow in the back of your head."

"A shadow?" I sounded like a nervous parrot, and my jaw dropped. My poor attempt at a smile was gone.

"Yes—we still don't know what it is, though. I don't want to tell you something unless I'm sure, so I will send you to a specialist."

"But . . . what do you believe it is?" I tried to keep a steady voice, but I knew I wasn't successful.

He looked down and kept opening and closing his hands. "As I said, I don't want to . . ."

"Could it be something serious? I mean, could it be something worse than a stroke?"

He looked like he was in pain and avoided eye contact. "I will fax your scans to St. Bernard's Clinic. It's a bit far away, so you should get someone to drive you."

He stood up, and it was obvious that the conversation was over. We shook hands, and his voice got more serious when he wished me good luck—it reminded me of someone preaching. I wondered if he was always talking to his patients like they were dying.

***

A week later I sat in another waiting room, only this time I was accompanied by my parents. The neurologist had called me himself and said that he'd received my MRI scans. He wanted to meet me and suggested I bring someone close. I didn't plan on it, but when I mentioned it to my mom, she and my dad booked a flight from Sweden straightaway. I was their only child, and even though they tried to hide it over the phone, I could tell they were worried. They'd also acted like that when I moved to another country for the very first time, even though that had been years ago.

***

In the waiting room, my mom pretended to read a magazine and my dad was glued to his phone. I sat between them and felt like a small child again. The atmosphere was tense. My feelings were all over the place—on one hand, I wanted to finally meet someone who could tell me what was going on, but on the other hand, I was terrified of what he would say.

The minutes passed slowly. I studied the people in the waiting room. Nobody was younger than sixty, which made my mood even worse. I wanted to stand up and scream, "I don't belong here! This is a big mistake, let me be." Instead I sat in silence and put my hands on my knees to prevent them from shaking.

The lady next to us looked fragile. I assumed the gentleman next to her was her husband, and they discussed something in low voices. I got the feeling that this was not the first time they had been there. They looked relaxed. Maybe I didn't have anything to worry about either. I prepared myself mentally, telling myself that the neurologist would inform me it was a mild concussion or the like, and that I would be back at work in no time. I tried to be positive. People made mistakes all the time, and doctors were just human.

The devil on my shoulder disagreed. *Of course you have something to worry about—why do you think they told you to bring someone close to you?* I went cold, and a dark cloud formed over my head.

The door opened, and an older lady came out with two younger women supporting her, one on each side. They all had the same hair color, and the younger ones seemed protective of the woman in the middle. I assumed they were her daughters. One of them stayed with the older woman while the other one went to pay at the reception desk.

The woman who stayed pressed the older woman's arm, and I could hear her say with a soft voice, "I told you he would have good news. Now let's just go home and rest."

I knew I should have been happy for them, but I couldn't help feeling a sting of jealousy. *Good for them*, I thought bitterly, and I got more and more nervous. I shook the negative thoughts away. *What kind of person am I?* I thought and felt embarrassed. There was no reason to be a bitch just because I was on the verge of a nervous breakdown.

I shut my eyes for a second. *Get it together!* I stood up to grab a fashion magazine, not because I had the slightest interest in the latest fashion deals right then but because it was a way to scatter my thoughts. I had started to browse through the pages without really looking when the door opened again.

A man in nice dark-gray pants and a well-ironed light-pink shirt put his head out. "Miss Larsson?" He waved us into the office, which was decorated in a minimalist way. Only a desk and three visitors' chairs sat in front of a big window. There were no paintings or plants. The view from the window was nice; it overlooked a grass lawn, some trees, and something in the background that looked like a small mansion. On the lawn a few rabbits were jumping around with no worries at all. The idyllic and peaceful view contrasted with the tense atmosphere in the room, which I guess was the whole point.

We sat down. I was between my parents again, as if they were trying to protect me.

The neurologist introduced himself as Dr. O'Brien. He was rather short, and almost disappeared behind his desk. He clasped his hands together and leaned forward.

"Miss Larsson, I have looked at your MRI scans." This guy didn't spend any time on small talk. "I'm glad you brought some family members with you; news like this can be pretty hard to take in at first." I started to feel dizzy. What exactly did he mean by that? He pointed at a screen on his desk and turned it toward us. "As you can see in this picture, there is a shadow in the back of your head."

There it was—a scan of my brain. I looked at it with fascination. The contours of my head were white except for a dark shadow approximately where the spine meets the head, in line with my ears. It was the size of a golf ball.

Dr. O'Brien cleared his throat. "I can't tell you now what it is. To be one hundred percent sure, we need a sample to do tests on." The hair on the back of my neck stood up. Sample? From my brain? I had to swallow the excessive saliva, and my nose wrinkled.

"But . . . what do you think it is?" My voice was shaking, and I was impressed he could even hear me.

"Well, I'm not going to lie to you. I'm concerned. Best-case scenario, it is a type of virus."

"And . . . worst-case scenario?" I wasn't sure I wanted to know, but I asked anyway.

"Well, it could also be a tumor." He paused and looked me straight in the eyes. "Either way, it is important we remove it as quickly as possible."

"Wait, what?" My head was spinning, and I tried to grasp what he had just said. I looked at my mom, and her watery eyes said it all—this was really happening.

I forced myself to look at the doctor again. "Tumor. Like in cancer?" I thought for a second I would faint and grasped the armrest.

"Yes, I'm afraid so. But we can't know for sure until we have removed and sampled it."

"But, but . . . it could be a virus, you said? How about a concussion? I did fall when I went skiing a while back. Are you sure we need to do something this drastic?"

He looked straight at me. "I'm sure. I would suggest we schedule you for the operation as soon as possible." He turned back the screen and looked at what I assumed was his calendar. "I can get you an appointment in two weeks."

Just like that. As if it were a dental appointment we were talking about. I stared at him without saying a word. I wondered if he was so distant because he had so many of these conversations, or if the man simply lacked feelings. My dad put a hand on my shoulder, as if he knew I was close to exploding. He smoothly took over the conversation and started asking all the questions I guess I should have asked. I was still in some kind of shock and gave him a thankful look for handling the situation for all of us.

A few minutes later, I reluctantly gave my credit card to the receptionist. My parents had offered to pay, but I didn't let them. I was used to taking care of myself, and I had no intention to stop now. When I saw the cost, I couldn't help feeling a bit annoyed, though. *Two hundred euros for a potential cancer diagnosis.* This Monday was not working out the way I had planned—that was for sure.

***

On the way home, I leaned my head back in the rental car and tried to take in the news. I had agreed to have the surgery in Dublin, and my mom was not happy with my decision at all. She wanted me to receive Swedish health care, but Dr. O'Brien had insisted that I have the operation as soon as possible. Mom knew as well as I did that I could not get treatment as fast in

Sweden. Best-case scenario, I would get moved up on a waiting list, but it would still be a waiting list.

I looked out the window at the cars passing by. Thousands of thoughts went through my head, and I tried to gather them. I imagined doctors opening up parts of my skull and got disgusted just thinking about it. I really hoped they knew what they were doing. I wondered when I'd be able to go back to work. I knew I probably shouldn't think about that right then, but the conference was coming up, and it was important that it worked out smoothly. I felt like I was losing control. All of a sudden I was not in charge of all my decisions anymore, and it scared me. I thought of the strict look Dr. O'Brien had given me. No matter how much I had tried to convince him that an operation probably wasn't necessary, he wouldn't give in. I usually never gave up, but this time was different. After all, I had to admit that he was the doctor, not I. I knew nothing about this, nor did I want to know. I felt a sudden need to scream, but I held it back. I wanted to disappear and pretend that this had never happened. A bad dream, that's all.

We sat in the backseat without saying a word. My dad gave me a pale smile and then avoided eye contact. He was never really good at handling emotions. My mom reached for my hand, and we didn't let go until the car pulled up at my apartment complex.

CHAPTER 8

A distant sound of voices brought me back to consciousness. The light was bright, and I blinked and tried to remember where I was. My throat was dry, and I really needed to visit the ladies' room. I opened my eyes and peered at the white surroundings. At first the light was too bright, but when my eyes got used to it, I could see a yellow drapery and got a glimpse of the room on the other side. Everywhere there were people in white uniforms hurrying back and forth. I tried to sit up but stopped immediately when I felt the pain in my head. I let my head slowly sink back into the pillow again. I looked down and saw that both my arms had tubes attached to them. I closed my eyes. A nurse pulled away the drapery and put her head in.

"Seems like somebody has woken up!" She smiled and got closer. She couldn't have been older than forty, but her ravaged face gave the impression she had been through and seen a lot in her days.

"Do you know where you are, love?"

I tried to shake my head, but it hurt too much.

"You went through an operation, and it went well. You are OK." She saw me glancing at the wires and said with a calm voice, "We're giving you a drip feed." She gently touched my arm. "Don't worry. You are in good hands."

I tried to sit up again, but she held me down. "Oh no. Don't be in a rush—it's best if you stay here for a while."

"I need . . ." My voice cracked. "Ladies' room." Those were the only words I could get through in a normal tone.

"Oh dear, I'm afraid that has to wait, too. I'll tell you what. I will put a bowl underneath you, and then I'll pull the drapery. You just press this red button when you are done, and I'll come and get it." She handed me a plastic wire with a big red button at the end.

My eyes became wide. Was she serious? Her face was blank, so I guessed it was not a joke. She disappeared and was soon back with the bowl she had been talking about. Great, there went the rest of my dignity. I did not have much of a choice, though; it must have been hours since my last toilet visit, and I could not hold it much longer. I filled the small bowl pretty quickly, and when I was done I pressed the button as instructed but nobody came. I tried to use my last energy to lift my hips up, but I got only halfway. So there I was, lying in my own piss, cursing the strained health care system. I knew it wasn't the nurse's fault. The hospital was just understaffed, and I guessed there were many other patients, too.

I felt like crying like a baby when she finally returned, and I hoped I never had to experience the same situation again. I thought of my grandma. She was living in a home for the elderly and got help with both her showers and toilet visits. I never thought of how that would affect her dignity, as she had been used to taking care of herself, having been a very independent woman her whole life. Well, now I knew. It's interesting how you never fully understand other people's situations until you walk in their shoes.

I dozed off, and next time I woke up my parents were standing by the end of the bed and looking at me.

Their worried eyes made me start crying, and I hated myself for it. I had always regarded tears as a sign of weakness, and I hated the fact that I couldn't keep it together these days. My mom stroked my cheek, and I could see a tear forming in the corner of her eye, too. "Everything will be all right." She repeated the phrase over and over, as if she were trying to convince herself as much as me. My dad didn't say anything, but his glassy eyes said it all. They stayed at a hotel close by, and I felt bad I hadn't had the operation in Sweden, where it would have been easier for them to visit. Oh well, the decision was made, and I couldn't change it now.

The headache started again, and I moaned. My instinct was to get up and run away from all of this, but my body didn't obey me. It was a terrible feeling not to be able to move. The nurse came back, and I swallowed the pills she gave me. I closed my eyes. I was not sure if it was the pills or just postoperative tiredness, but I was suddenly so sleepy. I tried to keep my eyes open but failed. I dozed off.

***

I don't know how long I was lying there. I went in and out of sleep, only to be given more pills that made me even more tired. The positive thing was that every time I woke up, the pain was a bit weaker. At one point they removed the drip feed and gave me some light food. I threw it up immediately, and then they gave me a break for a while. One day I managed to sit up and, with help from a nurse, walk the few steps to the toilet. I felt shaky and was happy once I was back in the safety of the bed again. Even though my progress was slow, I could see that I was getting better every day. My family was by my side the whole time, but I was too tired to talk. I wished they wouldn't look at me with those big eyes, like I was a hurt animal at a zoo. I knew they only meant well, and I did not have the energy to ask them to stop. My phone was buzzing constantly; my friends and colleagues were wondering how the operation had gone. It became tiresome to repeat myself, so at one point I wrote one message on Facebook to all of them, telling them I had no energy for visitors at the moment but promising to tell them more when I felt better. That resulted in fewer texts but more flower deliveries.

I lost track of the days, and it felt like I had been there forever when the turning point finally came. I managed to walk the steps to the toilet and back by myself, and I was as proud as if I had just run a marathon. The staff was not slow to move me to another ward. I guessed the bed I'd had was just for patients who'd come straight from surgery, and as soon as you improved they kicked you out. I didn't mind the change. I liked the new place better, as my room contained only me and another patient; there were almost ten patients in the last ward. This room had two big windows, from which you could overlook the garden outside. I had never been very fond of flowers and such, but after I don't know how many days of staring at the yellow drapery, I welcomed the change. I couldn't see the other patient, but I heard her snoring next to me, and soon I was sleeping, too.

CHAPTER 9

The drapery was pulled aside, and a lady with a sturdy frame grunted "Good morning" while placing a tray with breakfast on the small table next to me. To be honest, it sounded more like a growl than a greeting, and I guessed she had woken up on the wrong side of the bed.

My head felt heavy, and I rubbed my eyes before reaching for the remote. One press and I could lean back while the bed slowly moved upward. I stared at the tray and wrinkled my nose. I didn't feel like eating anything. Next to me the drapery was closed, but I could hear the patient on the other side. The sound that she now made left nothing to imagination. Gosh, did she never learn how to chew with her mouth shut?

I looked back at my tray. Scones, eggs, and fresh fruit. Not bad at all; maybe I should try to eat something. I forced down the food even though I didn't feel any hunger. I knew I had to eat to gain strength. Still slightly nauseated, I was relieved when the robust lady came back to collect the leftovers. I kept my tea and looked out the window. I heard the door open but didn't pay attention—after all, it was a busy place with nurses coming and going all the time.

My mom popped her head in and pulled a chair next to my bed. She told me that Dad had stayed at the hotel to catch up with some work but that he would visit the next day. I studied her in silence. Her light brown hair was cut in a nice page that framed her heart-shaped face. She didn't wear any makeup, and to be honest, she didn't need any. If you looked closely, you could see small wrinkles around her eyes, but why hide them? They were a result of many laughs, and I knew she was a strong believer in aging with dignity. Every age has its own beauty, and I was grateful for her genes.

"How are you feeling?" She tried to sound indifferent, but I knew her far too well to be fooled.

"Mom . . . they are taking good care of me."

She ignored my look of appeal and started to look for something in her big bag. I sighed when she pulled out a pen and notebook and started to write something down.

I knew there was no point in fighting her, so I prepared myself mentally to answer all her questions about the night, the medications I was on, and so forth. I knew she wanted the best for me and that she was leaving nothing to chance. She didn't trust the health care in Ireland at all and had decided to double-check every move with her hawk eyes.

When we were done she gave me a strange look, like she was trying to make up her mind. "I brought you something."

She pulled out a thin, cream-colored envelope sealed with a black bow and handed it to me. It looked clean and stylish, like someone had chosen it carefully. The only other time I had gotten something similar was when I'd received a wedding invitation two years earlier. The address was written in neat handwriting, and I was just about to open it when I noticed who the sender was. Mia Olsson.

A cold feeling spread inside me, like I had swallowed an icy drink that now slowly paralyzed everything in its way. I looked up at my mom to see if she knew, and her way of fidgeting with her long necklace said it all.

"Anna, I don't want you to make the same mistake as I did. I thought she deserved to know."

The icy drink in my throat now turned into hot tea on the verge of boiling. *How could she?* She was supposed to be on my side, and here she was contacting the one person I didn't wish to have in my life. I was furious, and if I could have left the bed I would have. As always when I got upset, the tears were not far away, and I desperately looked around for some distraction. I didn't like crying, not even in front of my own mom. It made me feel like I had lost control. She got the hint and stood up.

"I would read it, if I were you. It's not good to hold on to old grudges."

I stared at her. I still couldn't believe she had decided to be the messenger. "Thanks for ruining my day."

I then turned away, refusing to look at her on purpose, as I knew it drove her crazy. Her deep sigh showed that this time was no different. I swallowed to keep the tears away while she grabbed her bag and stood up.

"I'm gonna go and let you read in peace. I'll be back later, OK?"

I didn't answer, and when she left I threw the envelope next to the bed and picked up a travel magazine to scatter my thoughts. I browsed the articles about various warm paradise islands, but my eyes kept glancing over at the envelope that was lying all by itself on the floor. What had made her write after all these years? How did my mom get in touch with her when I couldn't? Would I finally get an answer to everything? The questions piled up with a crazy speed, and finally I leaned over the bed and reached for the only sign of life from Mia in fourteen years. I don't know how long I just sat with the envelope in my hands before I finally opened it.

My sweet Anna,

Do you remember I used to call you that? I know it was a long time ago, but if you just knew how many times I have started writing you but then stopped.

I am well aware that I owe you an explanation, but it still hurts too much. You have to trust me that I had my reasons, and I will tell you all about it when the time comes.

I'm sorry I didn't take your calls or respond to your attempts to get in touch. I got your letters, all of them.

When I look back at what happened, I believe I was in some sort of shock. It's not a good explanation, but it's true I had a depression shortly after I moved away. I hope you can forgive me one day.

You must be wondering why I'm writing to you after all these years. Your mom ran into my dad and told him what happened. My parents moved back a year ago—I guess they missed the land of Ikea too much. I'm still in Vienna, Austria, where I live with my soon-to-be husband, Franz.

Remember the letters we wrote about our future and hid in that small glade close to my house? They are probably all destroyed by now, but I still remember what they said. So many dreams! I was going to have a horse, three kids, and a handsome man... well, at least I got one out of three.

Anna, I really don't know what to say. When I heard what happened... it made me realize life is too short to live in the past. I'm truly sorry for what you are going through at the moment, and I hope you feel better soon. Life's not fair, and I'm so mad right now! It makes no sense that this happened to you, which is why I'm confident it will go away as fast as it came into your life.

You are strong, don't ever forget that. Even the strongest person needs some support now and then, and I hope you will let me visit you. Let me know the address and I will be on the next plane! I know we can't pick up where we left off, but I want to be there for you. Please let me know what you think.
   Yours,

   Mia

I slowly let the letter sink into my lap. My head hurt, and I suddenly felt so tired, as if I had not slept for a week. I resisted the urge to scratch the bandage around my skull and leaned back. There was a lot to take in, and I didn't know if I was ready for it.

Our childhood kept playing over and over in my head, like a repeat playlist. I closed my eyes and saw the two of us in the first grade on our way home from school, both dressed in colorful sweaters from Adidas. We had made up a game in which we were princesses who had escaped from home, and we couldn't be seen. Naturally, we had to hide every time someone came by, and the walk that would normally take fifteen minutes always lasted at least an hour.

So many nice memories, but they were shaded by the fact that she had cut all ties, with no explanation. One day I had a best friend whom I could tell everything, the next day I was left with no one. Thinking back on the day she told me she was moving, I got upset again—it was like no time had passed. After fourteen years, I still felt the same confusion and anger. The difference now was that I realized I couldn't blame her for moving. That was her parents' decision, and even if she could have told me sooner, it wasn't her fault. The big letdown was that she didn't reply to any of my letters or phone calls. In the beginning, my parents told me she probably needed time to settle in at her new place. That calmed me for a while, but when days turned into weeks and I still hadn't heard from her, I started to wonder. Did the mail system work differently in Austria, or had I gotten the wrong address? When I double-checked and it was clear I had written the address correctly, I felt like an abandoned puppy. I wondered why Mia didn't want to be my friend anymore, and I went through the last couple of weeks before her move in my head to try to find any signs. I figured I must have done something to upset her, but the more I looked into the memories, the more confused I got. We spent most of our waking time together, so if something had happened, I should have known. On the weekends, we were always watching movies together, or having sleepovers during which we gossiped for hours and ate popcorn till we were almost nauseated. I could count on my fingers how many weekends we hadn't spent together, the reason being to visit cousins or other family in different cities. Then we usually caught up for hours on Monday after school, going through every little detail of the time being apart. Looking back, I thought it seemed quite silly—how much could happen in a weekend anyway?

CHAPTER 10

The next day I had an oppressive headache. I felt like I needed water, but when I tried to sit up, a wave of nausea came over me. I gasped for air and reached for the alarm button. Within a few minutes, a nurse hurried in and asked how I was doing.

"My head . . . pain" were the only words I could get through. I tried to focus on the nurse's nametag, which said JAMES.

He opened up my file and looked at his watch. "Well, it's not time for all of your pills yet, but if you are in real need I can give you something for the pain."

"Yes, please." I managed to get up to an almost sitting position. I swallowed the pills before I sank back into the pillows again. I closed my eyes and tried to relax. Now it was a matter of patience. In only thirty minutes the pills would start working and I would feel better. I tried to think about something else and not focus on the pain. A memory of a beautiful glade popped up in my head. I had walked past it so many times when I was younger. Every time I went past it, it struck me how peaceful it looked, a small, flourishing piece of green lawn, no bigger than a bath towel. I'd grown fond of the place because it looked like it didn't belong there, in the middle of the forest with its tall trees. The rest of the grounds were pretty dry, but for some reason this little space flourished. The grass was not meant to grow there: the surroundings were dark, and barely any sunshine managed to get through the narrow firs. I had many times planned on taking a break there, bringing a book and letting the silence embrace me. Forget the surroundings for a while and become one with nature. I never got to it, though, always telling myself I was too busy.

My forehead pounded and brought me back to the hospital bed. I tried to massage my temples and glanced at the clock on the wall in front of me. Soon, soon, the pills had to start working.

The robust lady came in with lunch. She placed the tray on the small table next to me, but I couldn't even look at it. My stomach cramped, and it was like it screamed for food, but the nausea did not abate. I rolled over on one side. This was not working—what if I threw up here? The thought embarrassed me. I gathered all my strength and pulled myself up. I used the side of the bed as support before I staggered along toward the bathroom. It was just a few steps, but it was enough to make me short of breath. I stood in front of the sink and waited. My head was pounding, and my lips curled up in a disgusted shape, as if I had just bitten a lemon. I felt like my whole body wanted to get rid of something, and for the first time I actually welcomed an eventual vomiting. Everything was a blur of nausea and headache. I leaned forward, but nothing happened. After a while I gave up and held on to the wall while making my way back to the bed. I looked at the clock. One hour had passed since I'd gotten the painkillers, but I didn't feel the slightest relief. I whimpered and rolled over onto my side. There I was, gasping for air, when the robust lady came back to collect the tray. She looked at my untouched plate with chicken salad and surprised me by asking how I was feeling.

I wanted to scream, but instead I smiled apologetically and told her I'd been better. If there was something my parents had taught me, it was to be polite no matter the situation.

As soon as she left, I could drop the charade, and I tried to massage my temples while whimpering like a dog that had been left alone. I had never experienced this kind of pain before, and it felt like hours before James came back. He looked troubled when he realized that the headache hadn't settled down. He gave me my prescribed tablets and told me he would try to get ahold of the surgeon but that he would probably not be in for a couple of hours.

"Hours?!" I almost shouted. "Can't you give me something, anything?" He looked at me with a wrinkled forehead. It was like he first then realized the seriousness of the situation. I never asked for anything, so when I did—well, it usually meant something.

"You see, I believe the night staff gave you too few painkillers, especially since we stopped the steroids yesterday. That could be what is causing this. I would like to put you back on steroids, but I can't do it unless I have discussed it with the doctor."

I felt like hunted prey, with all my faith for an escape in James's hands. He must have seen the pain in my eyes because he suddenly changed his mind.

"Look, I'm gonna try reaching him on his personal cell, OK? Try to take it easy, and I'll come back soon."

The pain increased. I wiggled like a worm trying to escape a fisherman's hook, desperately trying to get away from the pain. I felt like somebody had put a wire around my head and was now pulling it as hard as he could. My eyes started to tear, and I got mad at myself. I knew the pain would get worse if I focused on it, and so I desperately tried to scatter my thoughts. After reaching for my cell phone and choosing a calm playlist on Spotify, I tried to relax. Maybe the smoothness of Joshua Radin's voice could put me to sleep.

It didn't work. As the minutes passed, the imaginary wire felt as though it were slowly cutting through my temples and leaving a thin, bloody mark like a crown around my head. The pain was so intense, I had to lift my fingertips to my forehead to check for damage, but it was dry as wood.

The light from the lamp in the ceiling was so strong, it stung my eyes, and I closed them faster than I could think. Thousands of thoughts swirled around inside my head, and I remember thinking that maybe now was the time when they would find out that the operation wasn't as successful as they first thought. Maybe they would explain to me that they'd done everything in their power, but it hadn't been enough. The fear took hold of me, and I rocked from side to side.

The hours passed like the motion of a snail. I reached for a plastic bag every now and then, when it felt like my stomach was about to turn itself inside out, but nothing happened. I tried to massage my own head, but the slightest touch burned as if there were an open wound. In my dizziness, I wondered if I had fallen asleep and somebody had cut my forehead with a sharp object.

James made frequent visits, and every time he looked more helpless. He couldn't get ahold of the surgeon, and he wasn't authorized to take his own initiative. His lips moved slowly, but no words came out. It was like he cursed in silence, and at one point I heard him complain to a colleague that if the night staff didn't start doing their job, he would quit. It blew his mind that he had to come to work and find patients in this condition. It wasn't right.

I whimpered and gasped for breath like an animal that hadn't gotten enough water on a hot summer afternoon. By the end of the day, I had almost stopped fighting, and I was starting to wonder if I would make it. I had never felt that way before, but I was seriously wondering if I had enough strength. *They'll get a free bed for someone else, though*, I thought bitterly.

The sound of a chair scraping the floor next to me got my attention. I hoped to God it would be the surgeon.

My mom's worried eyes peered at me.

"Hey, sweetie, what's happening? You look awfully pale."

The sight of her made tears start to pour down my cheeks. I could not control my emotions, and I had never in my life experienced such pain and hopelessness.

I let her take my hand and squeeze it lightly. She stroked my hair gently before standing up and rushing out into the hallway. I could hear how she caused a scene and screamed at the staff. "What is this? I thought it was a private hospital? This is outrageous and I will let the manager know!" Her voice had risen to a falsetto, and I could hear different voices joining in before I dozed off.

***

James woke me up by preparing a drip feed for me. "You are extremely dehydrated," he said without taking his eyes from what he was doing. "This will make you feel better."

A cold feeling spread through my right arm. I looked at the container with the solution that was disappearing unexpectedly quickly into my system. Was it supposed to move like that? He gave me two tablets and told me they had reached the surgeon and that he believed they must have been too optimistic when they stopped the steroids. Apparently my body wasn't ready for it, which resulted in the severe pain. I listened with only one ear and glanced at the drip that was now half-empty. He hurried off. The hospital must have been understaffed that day.

I turned my head to the window and saw that Mom was still there. Now that there was more space, she took a seat next to me. I pushed the button that moved me into a sitting position to be able to see her better. I got a sudden sickening feeling in my stomach and put my hand over my mouth. I tried to look for one of the plastic bags, but they must have moved them when I was sleeping. I tried to get up, but the drip wire was in the way.

Mom realized what was about to happen and jumped up from her chair. She ran off to get help while I gave the bed a last desperate look before it was too late. My stomach gave in. I leaned forward and let a cascade of liquid pour out of me. Mom came in again with James not far behind. He gave me a plastic bowl and helped wipe my mouth with a paper towel. Mom stroked my back and repeated, "Everything will be all right. It's gonna be OK," with a soft voice.

Wonderful, I thought before my next volcanic eruption. *This must be how it feels to lose all your dignity.* I felt like a helpless baby, without even enough energy to wipe my own mouth. My throwing up went on for a good few minutes, and I was amazed at how much one stomach could contain. The eruptions became less frequent, though, and after a couple of minutes I could lean back and close my eyes. James let me rinse my mouth with water before I collapsed on the sheets. I felt humiliated but relieved at the same time—at least I wasn't nauseated anymore. I pressed Mom's hand before I fell into a light sleep.

***

When I next woke, it was completely dark. I could hear the other patient snoring beside me. The metal wire I had imagined around my head had been exchanged for a soft hair band, still tight but not as bad as before. I let out a sigh of relief. Something moved beside me, and I realized that my mom was still sitting in the chair.

"How are you feeling?" When my eyes got used to the darkness, I could see that her eyes were filled with worry. Her forehead was wrinkled, and I recognized that expression—it was the same look she had given me years ago when I had woken up with nose blood all over my face and pillow. It happened every now and then when I had a massive cold and was nothing dangerous, but we didn't know that at first. Now I tried my best to give her a smile in an attempt to calm her down.

"Thank you." I seldom showed her the appreciation she deserved and felt a sting of guilt. She didn't respond right away, just pressed my hand and smiled at me.

"Shh, try to get some rest."

A single tear slowly ran down my cheek. I closed my eyes and let my dreams take me to the small glade in the middle of the forest, where the sunbeams were warming my face and it was completely silent.

CHAPTER 11

The next day the headache was almost gone, and I don't know if I had ever been more grateful.

A nurse I had not seen before came in and took my blood pressure. She told me that the surgeon would come for a visit later that day, but that they had already exchanged my medicine for a new, stronger one. "You are extremely dehydrated." She looked at me with big brown eyes. I liked her straightaway, as she seemed to genuinely care about my well-being, and I relaxed a bit. "I suggest we keep the drip for a while." It wasn't a question really, more of a polite statement. "When it's removed, it is really important that you get at least two liters of fluid a day, OK? We don't want you to ever feel as bad as yesterday again."

I nodded slowly. She didn't need to worry—after the previous day's escapades, I would do whatever they told me.

After breakfast, my mom and dad visited. They tried to remain calm while cursing the constraints many hospitals face nowadays. "I know they have loads of work, but this is not OK! Thank God that you feel better today," my mom said, stroking my forehead lightly.

I didn't say much, as my thoughts were wandering, but I kept coming back to a grateful feeling. I told myself to just imagine those who were in even more pain, a pain that would not go away. It struck me how little I knew about life. I remembered all the times when my mom had told me to be thankful that I had a healthy body that could move from A to B whenever I wanted. I used to put her off by saying that you couldn't go around life thinking that way, it wouldn't help anybody. Suddenly I realized that she had been right all along, and I promised myself to try to appreciate every single day from then on. I looked at the bruise that had started to form around the IV in my hand, and a dark thought popped up and reminded me that I wasn't healthy, so what did I actually have to be grateful for? I immediately shook that thought away. There would be a time when I felt better, there had to be.

"Anna, are you listening to what I'm saying?" My mom gave me the same look as when I didn't like her food.

"Oh, I'm sorry, I'm just so tired," I said, a bit guilty that I wasn't paying attention. The truth was, I had no idea what she had said for the last couple of minutes.

"Sweetie, no problem at all. You know what? I will leave so you get the chance to rest. I will come back tomorrow again, OK?"

I nodded and let her kiss me on the cheeks.

When she left I went back to my own thoughts. There were so many things I'd taken for granted. I thought back to the week before the operation, how I had been hurrying from one meeting to another with a constant worry that I wouldn't be good enough. I never gave a single thought to the fact that I could get out of bed quickly, bike to work, run around all day, and then more often than not squeeze in some time for the gym in the evening. The whole day without any pain. I wished I had given myself a break, thanking my body for all that it let me do, instead of feeling like I wasn't in the best shape. I swore to myself that this was something I had to start doing.

In the afternoon Nelly and two other friends came to visit. I hadn't wanted them to see me in this state, but at the same time, I'd missed talking to someone my own age. They had not stopped asking, and I had finally given in and said they could come.

In a few minutes they turned the boring hospital room into a lively coffee place. They had Starbucks to-go mugs in their hands, except for Nelly, who had chosen a green smoothie instead. There were not enough chairs, so the three of them sat on my bed and took turns cutting each other off. I looked down at my knee, where they had put different glossy magazines, and pointed out that one had a shoe special, which they'd thought I would like. I did—I probably had more shoes at home than all of them together!

I studied them and couldn't help smiling. They all had their own personalities: Nelly was our fitness guru, always preaching about the latest health trends. Alex, short for Alexandra, was our hipster and music junkie, always keeping us up to date about the latest concerts and festivals. Matilda was one with nature, and when we had first gotten to know one another she had tried to make us all go out hiking. By this point she had accepted that it wouldn't happen, not with the hangovers all the partying caused us.

"So... when are they letting you out of this shithole, Anna?" It was Alex who popped the question everyone didn't dare ask.

"Soon, I hope." I didn't know what else to say. "Are you gonna tell me all the gossip I missed out on, or what?" I said and winked at them. It was obvious I'd avoided the subject, but they let it slide, and soon they were talking all at once again.

They stayed a bit longer, but when I stopped being able to control my gasps, they kissed me on the cheeks and left, and

I could hear them still talking and laughing in the corridor on their way out.

I spent the evening browsing through the magazines and sinking in and out of sleep. It was scary how tired my body seemed to be. I noticed that someone had put the letter back on the table next to my bed. Every now and then it called for my attention, but I did my best to ignore it.

CHAPTER 12

Somehow the days passed pretty fast, even though I didn't do much other than have visitors and read magazines. Jasmine and William came together one day and gave me an update from the workplace, even though Jasmine pointed out that I needed to forget all about work and just focus on eating well and meditating. I slowly got back my strength, and at one point I could even leave the bed. My first walk outside in I don't know how long lasted for about five minutes, then I had to sit down and rest. *I used to run 10Ks without a problem*, I thought, and I couldn't help clenching my jaw tightly while gathering the strength to walk back to the hospital room. Every day I made improvements, however, even though all the medication made me tired. I would rather be tired than experience the pain again, so I swallowed everything they gave me like a good girl. I couldn't wait to get home to my own bed, but they wanted to receive the test results before they sent me home.

So one day it was time to see the surgeon again, and then be discharged. Once again my parents and I sat in the waiting room, only this time I had a big bandage around my head. I covered it up by wearing a big black hat, and I didn't care if it looked silly; I felt naked to show off my head in public, and I didn't want people to see what I had been through. So there we were, my mom and I browsing through magazines we had no interest in, just to pass the time. My dad walked nervously from one side of the room to the other. This time I didn't look at the other patients; I didn't want to meet their eyes, which I knew would be as nervous as mine. I just wanted to sit there in my own little world and pretend like it was nothing, like I was in a waiting room at the hairdresser's, waiting for my appointment. If I pretended like this wasn't happening, it was easier to deal with. I had browsed through the same magazine twice when the door opened and Dr. O'Brien called my name.

He was shorter than I remembered but exactly as stiff as last time. He closed the door and took his seat behind the desk. He put his hands together and leaned forward.

"How are you feeling?"

"Well, overall OK, I guess." I had forgotten his lack of emotions and got a bit upset. I mean, what did he expect? They had opened up my skull and done God knows what, but everything's just peachy. Never been better.

I tried to keep myself calm and not let my sarcasm show. It tended to surface when I was nervous, and it wasn't a trait I was proud of. He didn't seem to notice, though, and cut straight to the chase.

"As you might have understood, we have received the results from the tests. It took longer than usual, since they wanted to be absolutely sure." He paused to make sure he had our full attention.

"It was a tumor, as we expected, and it's called glioblastoma multiforme." By my confused face he must have realized we were not on the same page, so he translated. "That means it is a serious type of cancer."

I gasped for breath, and my head started to spin. My mom burst into tears, and my dad started to cough like he'd choked on something. I didn't bat an eyelid; it was like I was frozen, and I wondered how I would ever manage to get up from the chair. So many questions started to run around in my mind, competing for attention. Instead of one question after another, all of them came at the same time, like a barrage that had been let go.

"Are you sure? What does it mean? I mean, how serious is this?" I didn't even wait for his answers, I just let the questions I never thought I would have to ask pour out of me.

He rubbed his neck and raised his voice. "We are sure. To explain a bit more, there are four different types of brain tumors. Type four is the most serious one. Unfortunately"—he hesitated for a second and looked me straight in the eyes—"you have type four."

I heard a whining sound from my mom, who was now desperately looking for napkins in her bag to deal with the Niagara Falls she was the source of. She sounded like a wounded cat, and at first I didn't realize it was her. I turned and gave her a long hug. "It will be OK," I said, but I wasn't sure how convincing I managed to be. I was surprised by my own calmness, but I guess it was an unconscious decision to compensate for my mom's feelings. I didn't know how to react, but I had a strong feeling that one of us needed to remain calm right then, and it was sort of comforting to have found a task to cling to.

"What happens now?" I felt like I had to break the uncomfortable silence that had started when my mom ran out of tears.

Dr. O'Brien dropped his shoulders a bit, obviously relieved that we finally could move on. He might have been a great surgeon, but social skills couldn't have been required when hiring him. He lacked any signs of empathy.

"I recommend that you receive radiotherapy for six weeks. I would like to get you started with a daily chemo treatment at the same time. After those weeks, we will increase the dose of medication, but you will not have to receive it every day. We will schedule a new MRI, and hopefully the scans will show that you don't need further treatment."

"Hopefully?" I said a bit louder than I intended. I cleared my throat and continued, "I'm sorry, but I don't understand. I thought we removed the tumor. I was told the operation was successful! Then I can't have . . ."

My voice didn't bear up. I couldn't make myself say the word. I tried again. "I mean, I can't have . . . I can't be sick anymore." I couldn't take the word "cancer" in my mouth, it was like it had a bad taste. I looked at him with contentious eyes. I knew I was getting into deep water, debating a subject I had no knowledge of with a specialist, but I couldn't help myself. He waited for me to finish, and I could see that his lips were now pressed into a white slash, as if my questions were not even worthy of an answer.

"We have removed everything we can see, which is great. It might be that there are microscopic parts left, though, which is why we need to give you further treatment. It will hopefully be enough."

Could he stop saying "hopefully"? I was getting more and more frustrated with this man.

"OK . . ." I said hesitantly.

My dad put a hand on my shoulder and said, "What happens after the treatment? When can she go back to work?"

I held my breath, as I wasn't sure I wanted to hear what Dr. O'Brien had to say. He waited a bit before he answered. "Well, hopefully by that time the tumor has not started to grow again. In that case, you continue with your life like normal, though you will have to come here for regular visits every third month. But," he said, looking me straight in the eyes, "the situation is serious, and it is crucial that we start your treatment as soon as possible. The receptionist will book you in for your first radiotherapy session."

My lower lip started to shake a bit. I didn't want to ask what I was about to ask, but I had no choice. If I didn't, I knew it would haunt me in my dreams.

"How . . . serious is it? Will I die?" The last three words I almost spat out, like I wanted to get rid of them.

He opened his mouth and closed it again. He didn't get a second chance, since I cut him off. "Please be honest with me."

"Well, the average patient with this condition won't live longer than two and a half years from the day they are diagnosed. But your odds should be better. You are young and will handle the treatments better than someone with a weaker body. Plus, the operation was successful." He continued to talk about the kind of chemo I was going to receive, but I didn't listen any longer. Two and a half years? I don't know what I had expected when I set foot in his office, but it was definitely not this. My mom took my hand and pressed it gently. I did not say a word. I was completely empty inside and just wanted to get away from there. Away from this sterile office, away from the man in front of me who completely seemed to lack feelings, away from it all. I fixed my eyes on a couple of hares jumping around in the distance on the grass lawn outside. I heard my dad asking more questions, but I didn't hear what exactly he said. *Imagine being a rabbit*, I thought, *with no care in the world. Your biggest worry would be where the juiciest grass grew.* God, I was comparing my life with a rabbit's—what was wrong with me? Well, everything was better to think about than the reality right now.

I felt a light touch from my mom's hand on my arm, which brought me back to the room we were in. She helped me rise up, and it was like I had forgotten how to use my legs. We shook Dr. O'Brien's hand and left the office. After scheduling a new appointment with the receptionist, we slowly walked toward the lift. We went to the main entrance in silence and sat on a bench outside. My dad went to get my bags and order a cab. I leaned my head against Mom's shoulder. Now it was her turn to be the strong one. "It will be all right," she said and stroked my hair, careful not to touch the bandage. When the taxi came I went into the backseat without a word and let my parents give the driver the directions. I had longed for this moment, when I was finally allowed to go home. I hadn't counted on having such a weight on my shoulders, though. In the darkness of the cab it felt as though something released inside of me. I leaned my head against the window and cried in silence.

CHAPTER 13

Two weeks later, it was time for the treatment to start. The sooner the better, to increase my chances to live, as the surgeon so kindly put it. Sensitive guy, that one. The nurses explained to me that they would use radiotherapy to treat the area where the tumor had been, to prevent it from growing back. I couldn't sleep the night before and had twisted and turned in my bed. In a way it was good that they'd given me an appointment so soon; if they'd waited any longer, I would have had time to picture different scenarios, and with my imagination I would most likely have found hundreds of risks and reasons why I couldn't be on time that day.

The morning came, and even though my eyes were red from lack of sleep, the sensible side of me took over, and I went to the hospital by bus. I didn't have a car, and even if I did, I wasn't allowed to drive. My parents had returned to Sweden a few days earlier; they had already spent more days than their vacation policy allowed, and even though they'd wanted to stay, I insisted that they go back. I didn't want to put their lives on hold, and besides, I had always been good at taking care of myself. Slightly nauseated, I looked out the bus window and wondered if maybe this time I had been mistaken. Some things are hard to do alone. I stopped my thought then and there. What point was there to go through the operation if I chickened out now? I shrugged my shoulders and changed the song on Spotify. Almost there.

I was the only one getting off at the bus stop, and I imagined people judging me. I hoped they thought that I was a visitor, even though it felt like the word "cancer" was inked across my forehead. I adjusted the wig a bit, still not used to it and scared it would fall off at any minute. Of course, it didn't. I made my way through the entrance and toward the radiotherapy department. The receptionist smiled and showed me to the waiting room. She asked if I wanted some water, but I just grunted "No" without looking at her. Her kindness annoyed me, and I knew there was no reason for it. A less likeable side of me showed its ugly face when I got stressed.

I looked around. To my surprise, the room was filled with people, and since I was too restless to read anything, I studied the other patients. I had almost gotten used to being the youngest person in the room by then, but I still felt like everyone else was looking at me and wondering what I was doing there. I certainly looked out of place with my tight jeans, loose T-shirt, and turquoise Converse, plus the fact that I was young enough to have been everyone else's grandchild. Maybe it wasn't such a bad thing, though: if the statistics I'd read about my illness were based on this group of people, no wonder the life expectancy was so low. I bet the biggest challenge for these people was not the illness itself but the tough treatments. It gave me a small glimmer of hope. I was only twenty-eight. I should be able to handle this better than average.

"Miss Larsson?" A young woman no older than myself opened the door and showed me inside a long empty corridor. She told me to take off all my jewelry, and I went into a changing room to also remove my fake hair. I tried not to look in the mirror. Before the operation, parts of my head had been shaved, and I felt naked without the wig. I shivered. The situation wasn't helped by the fact that it was chilly in there. The nurse waited outside, and when I got out I felt ashamed to show my scar, even though I knew she probably had seen worse. I shook the vulnerable feeling away and followed her into a room where the entrance was blocked by a big warning sign. I came into a white and sterile place with no furniture except for some shelves along the walls. In the middle of the room a bed was placed with a big white machine hanging over it. It looked like a giant arm; it would have been great for any type of science fiction movie. The nurse helped me climb up on the bed, and reluctantly I placed my head carefully on a plastic pillow. The scar from the operation was still sore, and I did my best not to lean too much on it. A few days before, they had made a plastic mold of my face that I guessed would hold my head still. The nurses had worked efficiently and didn't seem to mind the seriousness of the situation. It had felt like I was at the dentist trying out new braces.

Another nurse joined in, and they started to make small talk a bit, I guess to make me calmer. Together they placed the purple mask on top of my face, and attached it to either side of the bed. My scar hurt when my head got pushed down, and I almost panicked when I noticed I could not move to release the pain. The mask had tiny holes in it, but I still felt it was hard to breathe, as it was too tight.

"Are you all right, love? I know it's not the most comfortable thing, but it will all be over soon, OK?"

She didn't wait for an answer, and I'm not sure I could have given her one with the mask on. I felt trapped and got a flashback from the movie *Face/Off* in which John Travolta's own face is cut off. Hopefully, that wouldn't happen to me. They spent quite some time adjusting my position and then left the room and turned off the lights. Some opera music started to play in the background, and I wondered if there really wasn't any other way to make the patients calm. Anything would have been better than classical music. It added to the feeling of being in a horror movie.

The white arm started to move around my head, and I could see a bright green light circulating on top of me. Now I understood why they'd put on the music—the machine was quite loud. I felt small and helpless, and I prayed to God that they knew what they were doing. After a while my breath calmed down, as if my body had accepted it was trapped and had decided to go with it. The buzzing sound made me almost fall asleep, and when the lights came back on I blinked in confusion. Was this it? The nurses rushed in and helped me get the mask off. Now, that was a relief!

"That wasn't so bad, was it? We had to take some scans today, tomorrow will be faster." The nurse had a thick Irish accent, and I had to focus to catch every word. She assisted me down and gave me back my belongings. My head felt a bit warm and tingly, as it should after having been radiated for the first time, I guessed. In the changing room I glanced at my own reflection in the mirror and realized I had a pale pink pattern of rectangles over my nose and forehead, an unwelcome gift from the mask. I damned the fact I hadn't brought makeup and tried to cover it with my hair, with no success. Oh well, I was soon to be home, and hopefully nobody would look at me closely.

On the way out I felt a bit dizzy and decided to take a cab. The receptionist waved good-bye and I smiled back, feeling bad about not being more polite before.

In the car I tried to gather my thoughts. It would be a hassle to go to the hospital every day for the next couple of weeks, but at least it wasn't as bad as I had imagined it would be. It wouldn't be my favorite way of spending time, that's for sure, but it was doable. I felt quite proud about how I'd handled the situation and started to scroll through my list of singer-songwriters in the phone. When I found Joshua Radin, I put the earplugs in and let his "Beautiful Day" enhance my mood.

I took out my notebook and made a cross in the calendar in the back. One down, twenty-nine to go. It felt like when I used to count down the days until Christmas as a kid—only this time, it wouldn't be as exciting.

CHAPTER 14

Somehow the weeks passed by, and I got used to going back and forth to the hospital every day. I wasn't feeling better, though; instead, I felt more tired every day. Apparently that was a normal side effect, and I couldn't wait for it to be over. The chemo pills made me nauseated, but thankfully the antinausea pills they prescribed kept it under control. Instead of lying with my head in the toilet, I was now just slightly queasy throughout the day. Suddenly I understood why cancer patients lose weight; it's hard to eat when the slightest smell makes your stomach move. At first it felt weird not to be at work every day, and I felt a bit isolated. Nelly brought me groceries, though, and I tried to see my friends as often as possible. I didn't have to come in to the hospital on the weekends, and I tried my best at those times to act as if everything were normal. The annual summer office party was coming up, and I didn't want to miss it for the world. My senior colleagues still talked about last year's lavish party, and this year's was supposed to be even more extravagant.

***

"Are you ready?" Nelly had to shout from the bathroom to make her voice heard over the music. We were listening to Rihanna while carefully preparing our makeup and trying on different outfits.

"Almost. I could leave in ten!" I shouted back and put another layer of mascara on. She didn't respond, and I figured she wasn't ready either. I took a step back and studied my reflection in the mirror. My dress was light blue with a floral pattern; I decided it was too girlie and added a black studded belt. The blond wig was shoulder length, which was longer than my normal haircut, and I wondered if anyone would notice the change. My closer friends had already seen it, and they all agreed it looked natural. I was still not convinced, since it felt like having a hat on. I didn't have much of a choice, though; the treatments had made most of my own hair fall out. I suddenly felt tired and had to sit down on my bed for a few minutes. I had ignored my pounding head for about an hour or so, but now I decided it was time for painkillers. When I passed the bathroom on my way to the kitchen, I saw that Nelly was still in her towel. What a wild preparty, I thought bitterly. Usually we would have had a few glasses of wine by then, and here I was, gulping water and fighting the urge to go to bed early. Nelly popped her head inside the kitchen and almost dropped her towel when looking at me.

"Are you OK, sweetie? You look awfully pale." She was studying me from head to toe.

"I'm fine," I said and swallowed two painkillers in one go.

The truth was, my head felt heavy, and I started to wonder if the summer party was such a good idea after all.

"OK . . . are you sure you want to go?" she said and scratched her arm nervously.

"I do, I'm just gonna rest a bit while you get ready."

I felt her skeptical eyes in my back as I returned to my room. Lying down on the bed, I tried to decide if it was the illness or the heavy painkillers causing my head to spin. I had to close my eyes to block out the light from the lamp. My thoughts swirled around like they were pieces of cereal in a big bowl that someone had just poured milk into. On the one hand, I knew I had to listen to my body, but on the other hand, I didn't want the illness to win. It had already taken so much of my freedom, and I didn't want to give it the pleasure of winning this battle, too.

After a while Nelly showed up in the doorway, looking fabulous in her crème-colored dress and leather jacket.

"I don't want to say it . . . but maybe you should stay home," she said and leaned her head against the doorframe. It messed up her curls, but she didn't seem to care. Her posture was out of sorts and her arms hung next to her like dead fish. She was clearly disappointed, but we both knew she was right. As much as I hated to admit it, my wild party days had come to an end.

CHAPTER 15

When the six weeks of treatment were over, I got one month to regain my strength—apparently I had reached the upper limit for how much a body can be put through. I decided to fly back to Sweden to be with family and just get a break from everything. When I got back to Ireland again, I would not have to receive treatment every day; instead, I would have one week of medication once a month. It almost sounded too good to be true—except that the medication would be much stronger than before. After reading up on the possible side effects, I suspected it wouldn't be pleasant.

Before I left, I invited some friends over to my apartment in Dublin. I was used to seeing them every week and was a bit worried they would forget about me. I knew it was a silly thought, but it was true I had missed out on lots of social events.

I had bought wine even though I had been advised not to drink. I wanted everything to be as before, though, and I even insisted on having a wineglass filled with Coca-Cola, so as not to stand out.

One of my fears was that people would treat me differently and tiptoe around me as if they were afraid I would break.

Therefore, I dressed up and put on makeup, even though I knew nobody expected it.

Nelly had helped me prepare some tapas, but since she added a healthy touch, I'm not sure the result counted as Spanish. There was no sausage or ham, since it had been claimed that processed meat causes some kinds of cancer. Instead we had pieces of tofu, but its loose texture made it hard to grab one without the tapas falling apart. To be honest, it didn't taste like anything at all, and to compare these small, sad white nibbles to smoked, salty ham would be a joke. I was happy she had made some other dishes, too, like the delicious skewers with mango, avocado, and feta cheese. It didn't take long before they were all gone!

When everyone had arrived and had gotten a glass of wine, I tapped my glass with a dessert spoon to get everyone's attention.

"Welcome, everybody! I'm so happy to see all of you."

There were no more than fifteen people, but when they cheered it sounded like a group of football hooligans. I took a deep breath and continued.

"I have only one rule for tonight: please don't ask me about anything health related."

Everyone reacted differently to my small request. Matilda looked like she would start crying; Nelly put her head to the side and looked concerned; and William put on the serious face he sometimes used when something went wrong at work.

Shit, I didn't mean to be a party killer, but by the look on everybody's face that's exactly what I was. Alex took the matter into her own hands. "Guys, I don't know about you, but I'm dying to try the tapas. Let's toast for a good time tonight!" She raised her glass, and everyone cheered. Alex winked at me, and I gave her a thankful smile. She sure knew how to work a crowd.

The evening was pretty calm, even though the sound level reached the same as a rather loud preparty. Aside from William, some other colleagues were there, including Jasmine. Most of the people were from outside work, though. Everyone seemed to have a good time, and I was happy I'd had a nap earlier. It would have been awkward for me not to have energy for my own gathering.

I spoke to everyone, and hugs were exchanged together with the usual questions about when I would get back to work. Since I had no clue, I answered as vaguely as I could.

At the end of the evening, I sat on the sofa together with Nelly and Matilda, and Alex tried to keep her balance on the unsteady footstool in front of us. The apartment was pretty small, and I realized we could use a few more stools and chairs.

"Guys, let's plan a trip soon! I'm dying to get out of this shithole," Alex said and had a big gulp of her red wine.

"Let's go somewhere sunny!" Nelly said, her eyes lighting up.

Matilda nodded, and we all started to shout out different travel destinations we wanted to visit.

"I know a national park in Switzerland that is supposed to be gorgeous," Matilda said, and she started to look for pictures on her phone to show us.

"Yeah, but it's not warm enough," Alex said quickly. I knew that was just an excuse for her not to go hiking. She preferred the big cities, and to be honest, I did, too. I didn't say much; I knew I couldn't plan anything too far ahead. The doctors had said I could go for a shorter vacation as long as it was to a country with proper health care, in case something were to happen. The tricky part would be to make sure we didn't travel when I was on chemo, and even if I wasn't, I wasn't sure I would have enough energy. My friends were pretty intense. *Just like I used to be*, I thought, and I wondered when the tiredness caused by the radiotherapy would go away.

William joined us, taking a seat on the floor with a glass of wine filled to the brim.

"Let's go to Barcelona!" Nelly suggested.

"Can we please have proper tapas then?" William said, smiling broadly.

Nelly looked like she wanted to punch him. "If you wouldn't be so traditional, you might actually find new favorites. I know for a fact that they have lots of juice bars there," she said with a loud voice and glared angrily at him.

William laughed; he loved to tease her because she was never slow to get upset.

"At least we know we need separate rooms for the two of you," I said and smiled.

"Or maybe they should be in the same room, to work things out?" Alex said, and both William and Nelly threw themselves over her and tickled her the best they could. She shrieked with laughter. I wondered what the neighbors would think and, even worse, if we would wake up our landlord, who lived in the same building. I took a sip of my Coca-Cola and realized I'd never thought of these things before. Was I getting boring? A sudden need to yawn answered the question, and I felt conflicted. I knew I had every reason not to be the same person anymore, but it scared me that I was changing this quickly. I wasn't used to the new person I was becoming and had not decided yet whether I liked her or not. Nelly seemed to notice that something was bothering me and gave my shoulders a squeeze.

"You OK?" Her carefully painted eyebrows got narrower.

"Yeah, I'm just getting tired." I held back another yawn and tried to smile. I wondered if I would have as many friends left when they discovered how dull I had become.

The thought scared me, and I felt a pressure over my chest, as if somebody had placed a dumbbell on top of it. The tears were burning in the corner of my eyes, and I blinked hard to force them to go away.

Nelly took my hand and squeezed it, which calmed me down a bit. She raised her voice to be heard over all the laughter.

"Guys, let's call it a night. I need to get up early tomorrow." She probably didn't, but I sent her a thankful thought for taking the hit. She didn't care what other people thought of her, and when a situation got tough, you knew she would stand by your side.

The others protested, but after a little more convincing from her they stood up. Alex commented that the wine was out anyway. There were a lot of hugs and "see you soons" before the apartment was empty again.

After they all left, Nelly helped clean up the mess we had made. While loading the dishwasher, I went over the evening in my mind. I thought of the way Alex had teased the others about getting a room, and I couldn't help smiling. Even though things were not the same, my friends always made me feel better. It was a welcome distraction to listen to their stories from their everyday life, and I would miss them like crazy in the coming month.

PART 2

CHAPTER 16
Sweden, August 1994

I looked at myself in the hallway mirror. The first day of school had finally arrived, and I wanted everything to be perfect.

My normally dark blond hair shimmered in different golden tones after all the hours in the sun that summer. I removed a piece of hair from my eye. I wore a red hoodie with the alphabet on it, even though they could have been Greek letters for all I knew. I recognized the *A* and the *N*, though, since my parents had taught me how to write my own name. I flattened out my skirt, which had already gotten wrinkled.

"Anna, you ready?"

My mom showed up in the hallway and stopped when she saw me. "Aw, you look so pretty," she said and kissed the top of my head.

I wished she would stop talking and put her jacket on instead. "Shall we go?" I said and went to open the door. I didn't want to be late and started to jump up and down on the spot until she finally locked the door behind us.

When we arrived, my mom followed me into the classroom. I glanced shyly at the other kids, who had already started to look for their seats in the narrow room. I realized that most of them didn't have their parents with them, and I quickly kissed my mom good-bye. Slowly, after a bit of fumbling, I joined in the search for a seat with my name on it. I found it pretty quickly and gave a sigh of relief. Hopefully there were no more kids with the same name. My backpack had to go on the back of my chair. I sat down, happy to have completed the first task, when a shrill sound broke the silence. Surprised, I turned around to see that it wasn't an alarm. Instead it was a small girl looking like she wanted to hit me. Her eyes flashed like lightning.

"You are sitting on my jacket," she said and pulled something from the floor so hard my chair almost fell.

I looked at her in surprise, then looked down and realized she was right. My chair was placed on top of her jacket, which must have slipped and ended up on the floor.

"I'm so sorry," I said, and my cheeks turned red in a heartbeat. I jumped down and lifted my chair so she could pull out the piece of yellow fabric that was stuck.

"It's brand new, and I only got it if I promised not to stain it. So thank you very much." She stared me down till I turned away. Her fragile appearance didn't seem to go with her attitude. Her light red hair hung in two braids on each side of her face. I suspected it was the sun that had brought out the freckles that covered her nose and cheeks. I was jealous—I had always wanted freckles of my own, and I smiled at a memory of when I had used a pen to paint tiny spots on my own face. My mom had been furious.

"Mia," the girl said with a clear voice that woke me from my thoughts. She must have noticed that I wasn't focused and went on a bit louder. "My name is Mia. What's yours?"

"Oh. It's Anna." I smiled. "But I always wished for a cooler name, like in the American movies."

"There is no rule that says you can't have two names," Mia said with a mischievous smile. She surprised me once more. I had never thought of that. I opened my mouth to ask if she had more names, but I never got the chance. The woman who I assumed was my teacher rang an old-fashioned bell till we all sat in silence looking straight at her. She was a solid woman who introduced herself with authority. Her name was Eva, and I got the feeling it was best not to mess with her.

The rest of the morning passed quickly. We introduced ourselves, told a story from the summer, and colored our name signs. When it was time for lunch, the whole class went in a line to the canteen, holding hands. Eva had an almost military bearing, and I couldn't decide if I was scared of her or not.

The canteen was loud and messy, and I felt as if the older kids looked at us like hungry wolves. Nothing seemed to frighten Eva, though, and she showed us around like it was her home. In some strange way I liked her, as she felt calm and safe, and I figured it was best to keep close. By the end of the day, we all got a yellow cap with the number one printed on it. Now we were officially enrolled in the school! Some of the kids put their caps on backward, so they would look like rappers in a music video. I glanced at Eva's disapproving face and then decided it was probably better to place mine the way it was supposed to be. They gave us a schedule for the rest of the week right before a bell rang. Time to go home!

I started to walk home, humming a song I had heard on the radio that morning. I couldn't wait until the evening, when I would tell my parents all about the day.

"Hey, little bug, stop!" At first I didn't understand that the voice was talking to me. When the shouting didn't let up, I stopped and slowly turned around. A tall boy came walking toward me, with two friends not far behind.

"Why are you in such a hurry?" The boy came closer and studied me from head to toe. He had dark, almost black hair, and his crew cut made him look like he belonged in the military. I had never been good at guessing people's ages, but he was definitely older than me, maybe twelve. He had a scar across his left eyebrow, which I assumed had come from a fight. I swallowed and took a step back.

"I . . . I'm just going home." My voice sounded so small in comparison with the guy, who was at least two heads taller than me. The three of them grinned.

"You are new here, right?"

There was something about this guy that made me nervous, and I could only nod. It was like my voice stopped working, and I looked down at my shoes.

"There is something you should know. You are nothing the first year, nothing. Do you understand me?"

I could still not manage to talk to him and could feel his eyes on me. When I didn't reply, he raised his voice.

"I said 'Do you understand?!'"

I slowly raised my gaze and whispered, "Yes."

"You need to know that inside the classroom it might be the teacher that's in charge . . . but out here it's me, OK?" He smiled scornfully. "Once you set your foot out here, you are mine." He smacked his lips, apparently happy with the effect he had on me.

"You can tell your little friends, too. My name is Peter. Don't you forget that." I looked around, wishing he would let me go.

"What is it, little ant? You don't like our company?" He turned to his friends and put out his arms. "Guys, seems like this little cockroach doesn't want to hang out with us anymore."

One of the other boys started to laugh. He was not as tall as Peter and a bit overweight, and his swollen upper lip indicated a person not afraid of conflict. "I think she will start crying!" His laugh sent my body shivering. How did I end up in the middle of this?

I bit my lip, determined not to give in to the burning feeling behind my eyelids. When I didn't seem shaken enough, Peter became restless. He walked a lap around me, and I didn't dare move or breathe.

"Take off your backpack."

My shoulders got stiff. "But . . . it's new."

"Excuse me, did you say something?" He came closer. "What is it that you don't understand? When I say something, you obey." He was now so close I could smell his bad breath. He had apparently liked the fish we'd had for lunch. His voice was now louder, and his face got red. I took a step back and accidentally stepped on one of his friends, who immediately saw an opportunity to get a steady grip around my ponytail. He pulled hard, while another one tore the bag off my back. Tears started to form in my eyes, as his grip was so firm that it hurt. Peter leaned forward.

"That wasn't so hard, was it?" He grinned and showed his uneven teeth. He opened the bag, then turned it upside down so all my pens went flying all over the pavement. Peter stepped on the painting I had made that day. I was going to give it to my parents, and now it was covered in mud. He smiled his stiff smile that made him look like a woman on Botox, and held up the backpack.

"Not bad at all. Perfect for my little sister. How nice of you to think of her." His smile broadened when I tried to move away from his friend, which resulted in an even tighter grip around my hair.

"Stop it!"

A sharp voice from a girl cut through the air like a loud bell. I couldn't move, and my face was now turned upward so I could not see her, but there was no doubt it was the same voice from that morning. Peter licked his lips, and his eyes narrowed as he studied the tiny girl approaching him.

"And who do you think you are?" His voice sounded more like a growl now.

She put both hands on her hips and stared back at him with stubborn eyes. "I'm her friend. Let her go."

He looked at the tense little girl in front of him, obviously taken aback by the way she dared to talk to him. Everything went silent, and it was like he was trying to decide what to do with this new situation. Then he smirked, and the corner of his upper lip twitched before he burst out laughing. The grip around my hair loosened up a bit when his friends joined in. Peter wiped away a tear from the corner of his eye. When he finally calmed down, he looked at his friends and winked.

"Today's youth." His voice was ironic, and I could tell that this was the calm before the storm. He took a few fast steps toward her, and before we knew it she was lying on the ground, bleeding from her hands where she had tried to stop the fall. When she started crying, he smiled with malicious delight and put his hands on his hips. He licked his lips slowly like I had already seen him do a few times and tossed his head. "Let's go." The three of them ran away with their new possession while I went over to Mia.

"Are you OK?" I helped her clear off the leaves from her jeans. She dried her tears and nodded.

"Such a pig." Her voice was filled with disgust. "He must be like five years older or something."

She made an attempt to imitate a pig, pulling her nose up and starting to jump around in a circle, grunting. I couldn't help bursting out in a big laugh, which was liberating after the tense afternoon. Then I noticed stains of blood on her jacket and immediately got serious.

"Oh no, look!"

She looked down, and her eyes got bigger. "My parents will kill me!" All of a sudden she didn't look as tough anymore. I got an idea and looked around for my yellow felt-tip pen. I found it under a leaf and helped her cover up the damage the best I could. It wasn't perfect, but it was better than before. She gave me a big smile, and together we collected the rest of the colored pens, erasers, and papers from the ground. I glanced at her. What would have happened if she hadn't shown up? I shook that unpleasant thought out of my head, and we started walking home together.

When we were almost at my house, she showed me a shortcut between the trees, a small path that was hard to see from the road. I stopped for a bit and admired the little glade opening up in front of us. How beautiful it was! Tall birch trees formed an avenue around the almost overgrown path, dark except for the small strings of sunshine that managed to get through the thick branches. It was a hidden place, and I wondered why I had not been there before. We jumped up on an old stone wall and took a break. There we were, dangling our legs and talking about everything and nothing. The memories from the afternoon faded slowly. Mia seemed easy to talk to, and the hours flew by quickly. I enjoyed her company when she suddenly jumped up.

"Oh no! I promised to go straight home. My parents might be worried." I had no idea how long we had been talking but realized we must have been there for quite a while. Together we hurried through the woods and helped each other hold branches that were in the way. When we came out on the other side, the light was too bright at first. After our eyes adjusted, we continued and did not separate until we reached the playground not far from my house. I went to the right and she to the left, but before she disappeared I turned around and shouted her name. She turned around on the spot and almost fell. I waited a few seconds to find the right words, but it seemed harder than I thought.

"Thanks, for you know . . . today."

She gave me a broad smile that showed her two dimples, one on each side of her small mouth. "No problem." She did another impression of a pig before she turned around and galloped away.

That night I couldn't sleep. There were too many new memories from the day that had passed, and I twisted and turned under the duvet. My blood went cold when I thought about Peter and his two friends. I felt better when I thought of Mia, my new friend and savior. If I'd only known then what an impact Peter would have on both our lives, I probably would not have been able to sleep for the whole week.

CHAPTER 17
Sweden, 2015

It felt great to be home. I had decided to stay at my parents' house in the south of Sweden, and it wasn't long before they were treating me like a kid again. A year ago it would have driven me crazy, but all the things that had happened during the previous few months had made us closer, and I didn't mind their help. I finally acted like I always should have, with gratefulness instead of impatience. Family was the most important thing in life, I realized now, and I had tended to forget it. It was like I had gotten a new pair of glasses and finally could see clearly. Instead of an annoying older couple limiting my freedom, I now saw two loving human beings who only wished the best for me. They had given me so much time, love, and care during my childhood, and it struck me that I had never thanked them properly. I made a mental note that, if I lived through this disease, I would take good care of them when they were too old to handle everything themselves.

To eventually move back to Sweden had not always been an obvious choice. A year earlier I'd had a conversation with some friends from the company in which we discussed if we would ever move back to our home countries. All of us came from different parts of the world, but we had a lot of things in common; the most visible was that we'd left our homes to find bigger cities, bigger challenges, and greater careers. We were all hunting for something better, and none of us had any plans to move back in the near future. We didn't even consider that "something better" actually could be found much closer than we thought.

"Coffee?"

My mom's clear voice put an end to my daydreams. She had taken the day off, and she now stood next to my lounge chair in the garden with two cups in her hands.

"Sure." I pushed my peaked cap back a bit to be able to see her better. I normally didn't wear hats and such, but I wasn't allowed to be out in the sun if I didn't cover the scar. It was a nice summer day, and for Sweden it was pretty warm. I even had shorts and flip-flops on. I put my book away when she handed me one of the cups. She sat down in the chair next to me and lifted her eyes toward the sun. It was funny how we acted when the sun came out in this country. People stopped in the middle of the street and turned their heads toward the sky, to bask in the sunlight. It was even more noticeable when spring was approaching after a long winter, but we sometimes did the same during the summer.

"I ran into Mia's parents again the other day."

She let the sentence hang in the air, as if she expected an outburst from my side. We had not discussed Mia since my mom had brought me the letter. Since then, I had had a lot of time to think, and I would be lying if I said that Mia hadn't crossed my mind several times since. I still hadn't written her back, though. Every time I tried, it was like something was blocked, and the few sentences I scribbled down would end up in the wastebasket. I started to get a feel for why she had not written sooner—it wasn't that easy.

I moved the cup around in my hands, not sure what to say. It was true that most of my anger was replaced by curiosity, but I wasn't sure how to deal with it.

"Yeah? How are they doing?"

"Good, they are happy to be back. Especially her mom; she has always been fond of Sweden."

Then they shouldn't have moved in the first place! My old anger surfaced for a second, but I pushed it down again. I realized it would only eat me from the inside if I didn't stop, and it just wasn't worth it anymore.

"Did you ever write her back?" Mom tried to sound indifferent, like she was asking if there was milk left or not. I could tell she was eager to know, and I decided not to keep her in the dark.

"No. I mean . . . I've tried, but I don't know what to say, really. It feels so weird when you're not face-to-face."

My mom took a sip of her coffee and let out a small humming sound, as she always did when she was making plans. When she did, it was best not to disturb her, and I turned to the sun again. The warmth felt so good on my pale skin, and I almost dozed off. After a few minutes my mom sat up straighter, and I could feel her eyes on me.

"What if . . ." She stopped in the middle of her own sentence and disappeared in her thoughts again.

"What if what?" It was annoying when she cut herself off!

"What if . . . you invited her over?"

I started laughing but had to stop when I saw her stony face. Was she serious? "Oh. You're not kidding?"

"Think about it—you used to be inseparable. That kind of friendship doesn't come around every day. Isn't it about time you bury the hatchet?"

"It is. But to have her here . . . I mean, we don't really know each other anymore. It's been like what, fourteen years?"

"Worst-case scenario, you don't get along anymore. Although I doubt it. I've never seen two kids in better symbiosis."

I thought back to all the fun we'd had together, and I couldn't help but smile when I remembered the time we had picked cherries from the neighbor's garden. We'd both gotten covered with dark red stains, and it was no mystery who the guilty ones were.

To be honest, I never had a friend who understood me the way she did, who laughed at my stupid jokes, and who stood up for me no matter what the situation. Oh, how I missed her!

"I guess I could at least invite her. Maybe she won't even show up."

***

She did show up. One phone call and her flights were booked. She had lots of vacation days left, and even if she hadn't, she assured me that she would have found a way to visit. Some things were more important than others. It felt weird to hear her voice—it now had a slight undertone of an Austrian accent and the phone call was quite stiff, but what did I expect after so many years? I convinced myself it would get better when she arrived.

As soon as my mom heard the news she busied herself in preparations and started to clean the whole house, even though Mia would be staying at her own parents' place. I helped her a little but slept most of the time, as the radiotherapy had really taken its toll. When I was awake I wandered around the neighborhood, visiting my old school and looking at photos from when I was a kid. Most of the pictures were of Mia and me, and it was fun to see how we got older but still goofed around.

There were photos of us playing with Barbie dolls, swimming in various lakes in the summer, reading next to each other in my parents' garden, and then later on, our first horseback riding lessons. I found an old school calendar from our second year; we must have been eight years old. Mia and I were sitting next to each other in the first row, and I was laughing while all the other kids were looking straight at the camera like they were supposed to. I remembered that day. Mia had said something really funny just before the camera went off, and I couldn't help but burst into laughter. I browsed through photos of the other classes and came across the older kids. I looked for a specific name and swallowed hard when I found it. Peter was standing in the back because of his height and grinning broadly. I wondered what ever happened to him. *He's probably making life harder for his coworkers*, I thought, and got a bitter taste in my mouth. There were so many times he had made me and the other students miserable, and it was a relief when he finally graduated. Just looking at him made me upset, as though no time had passed. I closed the calendar with a smacking sound. I couldn't stand the memories he evoked. I put away the calendar in the bottom of the box with my photos and decided to pick just a few to show Mia when she arrived.

CHAPTER 18

A few days later I was out walking with my dad. He told me about his company's latest business issues and challenges. I didn't say much, but he didn't seem to notice. We usually had long discussions about the differences in the business landscape in Sweden and in Ireland. He valued my fresh ideas, and I enjoyed listening to his experience. Something had changed, though. I wasn't as interested anymore. Lately I had started to doubt my own career path; it no longer seemed important.

"So when are you starting your own company?" he said, and the sudden question forced me back to reality again.

"One day," I said and gave him a pale smile. I used to bore him with new crazy business ideas every time I came to visit. Now I got a bit annoyed, since he knew very well that I couldn't make any long-term plans at the moment. He put an arm around my shoulders, and I held back an impulse to snap at him. I knew it was his way of saying that he believed I would get well. Maybe I had gotten my positive thinking from him.

I looked at my watch and realized we needed to turn back if I was going to be home when Mia arrived.

***

The doorbell rang one, two, and even three times before I finally got up and slowly went to open it. This was it. I was about to see Mia for the first time in years, and I would be lying if I said I wasn't a bit nervous. Would I recognize her? Could we put all that time behind us? What if we didn't get along anymore? There were so many questions that I hoped she would shed some light on. Before I opened the door, my hand went up to the back of my head, to where the wig covered the scar. I wished we hadn't been meeting under these circumstances, when my energy levels were drained. Hopefully she wouldn't stay long.

At first we didn't say anything. She stood like a ghost in the doorway with a bunch of flowers clutched tightly in her hands. I couldn't move or say anything. It was like all my words were glued to my throat, and they didn't move in any direction.

We stared at each other like it was the first time we were meeting, and the minutes passed by slowly. It would have continued that way if my mom hadn't shown up behind me. Her whole face lit up, and I moved so she could give Mia a big hug, as I should have done if I hadn't been paralyzed.

"Oh my goodness, how beautiful you are! It's so nice to see you again! Come, come, let me put those in water."

I barely looked at the gift, and I didn't thank her. I was grateful that my mom was there to make Mia feel welcome, as I apparently had lost all signs of decency. My mind went round and round. So many tears I had shed because of the girl in front of me, and I was still confused. Why had she left? And, most important, why had she come back?

I studied her in silence while Mom put the flowers in a vase. Mia's characteristic nose was the same, pointing a bit upward, which made her look stubborn. She was thinner than I remembered. She had always been slim, but at our age most people had gained some extra pounds, or at least gotten bigger hips. Her lean face revealed a few wrinkles and made her look a bit older than she actually was. She was still beautiful, though, and with her shiny hair in a strict hairdo and carefully painted lips she looked almost like a movie star. I noticed she had colored her red hair and could now be taken for a blond. Only the freckles revealed her true nature. She had a slight tan, and I couldn't help wondering if it were real. She had always just been white or screaming red, nothing in between. Either way, she made it work, and it looked good with her white cardigan and discreet silver jewelry. If I had only one word to describe her, it would be "elegant," and the T-shirts and cords that I remembered were long gone. I felt a bit underdressed in my jeans and oversize shirt.

"I'll let you girls be alone; I bet there is a lot to talk about." Mom quickly disappeared and left us alone in the kitchen. Mia took a seat by the table while I looked for cups in the cupboard.

"Tea or coffee?"

"Coffee, please." She looked out the window and fiddled with the purple tablecloth. Neither of us spoke, and the atmosphere reminded me of the one you find after a funeral, when people are afraid to say something inappropriate.

All the cups were different, and I chose a cream white one for her and a bright pink one for me that said "Good morning, beautiful, you can do it!" God knew I could use some encouragement right then. I prepared the coffee a bit more slowly than usual to buy myself some time. As long as I had something to do I felt it was OK not to say anything.

She must have gotten tired of my silence, as she cleared her throat and let go of the tablecloth.

"I understand if it's weird that I show up like this." She paused and rubbed her chest like she was in pain. It was obvious she was uncomfortable, but I was determined not to make it easy for her. She looked up at me, then quickly away again.

"I'm sure you don't even want me here. But when your mom told me what happened . . . I just had to come and see you."

My lack of words became awkward, and I decided to try some small talk. The serious topics could wait a bit longer.

"When did you arrive?"

"Yesterday." She smiled and looked relieved. "It's pretty fast nowadays, especially with the bridge from Copenhagen. The flight itself was not even two hours."

I poured the coffee and put down the white cup in front of her. The cream tone matched her outfit perfectly. I sat down opposite her and blew some air into my cup. She leaned forward and touched my arm slightly. "You have to tell me if you want me to leave." I twitched and pulled my arm away.

She looked hurt but didn't say anything. Her shoulders dropped, and she started to bite her nails, just as she'd done when we were kids. When she finally stopped she shook her head and looked up.

"I just felt . . . it's been too long, Anna. God only knows how many times I have thought of writing to you but never did. When I found out about your condition, I was ashamed. You were my best friend, and I should have known without anyone telling me. I'm ashamed." She said it with emphasis and looked at me with sad eyes.

I didn't say a word. Inside my head my thoughts were swirling, and I wanted to scream that I had missed her so much, that I hadn't eaten for a week when she went away, that I'd missed her so many times it hurt even trying to count them. I had never met anyone like her during the fourteen years that had passed. My pride stopped me from letting her know what I felt. I couldn't say anything at all. It was like I had something in my throat that blocked all the words that should have been said, and I couldn't do anything about it.

Mom came in and broke the tense silence. She apologized and reached for a notebook she'd left on the counter. I don't know whether she'd left it there on purpose to have an excuse to check in on us.

I stood up to get some milk for the coffee. Mia looked out the window again, deep in thought. Mom seemed to feel the tension and left the room quickly. As soon as she left, Mia turned around and studied me, her eyes on my wig. Everyone seemed surprised that it looked so real; maybe they expected a price tag or something.

"Are you in pain?"

"It's OK. After all the drugs they fed me, I don't feel much," I said bitterly.

"I trust you will tell me if you want to rest." She hesitated.

Now the ball was in my court. It would have been so easy to say yes. Then I could have pretended like nothing had happened, that this had just been a dream from my past. When I saw the gleam of hope in her eyes, I began feeling guilty, though, and softened up. I shook my head, and it made her smile so big her dimples showed.

I sat down again and decided that I had punished her enough. But if we were going to get somewhere, I had to put all the cards on the table.

"Look, I'm still upset you just disappeared like that. For a fourteen-year-old, that was hard to accept. I guess you had your reasons, but I didn't know what they were."

"I know, I know. And I'm sorry."

"Now that you are here . . ." I looked at her and could feel a smile forming in the corner of my mouth. "I'm just happy to see you."

She smiled back, and I took her hands. For a moment we just sat there, and I remembered that if it weren't for my illness, we would probably not have been talking right then. It was horrible really, how people postponed important things in life until it was almost too late.

Once we started talking, we couldn't stop, just like when we were kids. I told her the most important things that had happened but made it clear that I didn't want to talk about treatments and possible cures. Everybody seemed to be an expert on cancer cures lately, and I was amazed at how much advice I received each week. I just wished everyone would stop treating me like a victim—I knew I might die, but that day was not today. It wasn't long until she started crying. That was the kind of person I remembered she was, tough as nails on the outside but soft on the inside.

When she calmed down, she said that she respected my wish and then smoothly turned the discussion to her own whereabouts. I learned about the fiancé whom she'd met about two years earlier when she took a scuba-diving course. It didn't take long before they booked a diving trip together to the Maldives, and they had been inseparable ever since. He worked as a banker in the business district of Vienna, born and raised in the city. She was a project manager at a company arranging conferences and business events and was almost married to the job. All in all, she seemed busy but happy. I glanced at the ring on her finger; it looked expensive. As she described their wedding plans, I couldn't help but wonder if she meant to invite me to the wedding the following year. Probably not, and I felt a bit hurt. Ignoring it, I asked about Vienna, her parents, and everything else that came to my mind and did not involve her leaving. We would get to that topic sooner or later, but right now I was simply happy that we had found a way back to each other, and I wasn't going to spoil it just yet. We lost track of time but must have been in the kitchen for hours before I tried to hide a yawn with the back of my arm. It wasn't very smooth, and she wasn't slow to respond.

"I'll let you rest." She jumped up from her chair and put our empty cups in the sink. I got up, too, and we both hesitated, just for a second, before hugging good-bye. "Can I come back again soon?"

I nodded eagerly and apologized that I didn't have the same energy as before. When we were kids we would stay up all night talking and laughing. She assured me it didn't matter and that she had to spend some time with her parents anyway.

When she was gone I went up to my old bedroom, where my posters of horses still covered most of the wallpaper. I lay on my bed, looking up at the ceiling, trying to make sense of everything that had just happened. All this time I had painted a picture in my mind of a girl who had betrayed my trust, but now I wasn't so sure anymore. Mia was just like she used to be, and she did seem genuinely happy to see me. That told me that I had not done anything to make her cut all ties, as I had first thought... but then what were her reasons?

CHAPTER 19

The next day I was home alone, and I enjoyed the silence while having my morning coffee. When I looked out the kitchen window, I realized that one of the cars was still in the driveway. My parents must have shared a car to work. I bit my lip, and my heart started to beat faster. I knew I shouldn't drive because of my impaired vision, but here in the countryside there wasn't much traffic during the weekdays, if you didn't count a tractor or two. I had always loved driving, and I really felt like getting away. I decided it wouldn't hurt to take the car for a short spin, and I quickly finished the coffee.

A while later I was stepping on the gas pedal, curious about what speed I could push the small car to. It felt liberating to get out of the house, and I enjoyed the view of the open fields on both sides of the road.

Driving cleared my head, and I always got my best ideas when I was behind the wheel. I felt calmer than I had in a long time. When I thought about it, I realized that I'd been more relaxed than usual ever since I was put on sick leave. It was strange, since I had a lot more important things to care about nowadays. Maybe that was part of the reason. Without noticing, I had let go of many small worries. Things like being late or not being on top of my game all the time didn't bother me as much anymore.

Work seemed far away, and I wondered how I could have let stress cloud my mind like that. I got mad at myself, even though I knew it wouldn't help. I swore to myself I would do things differently when I got back from sick leave.

Before the illness I'd seldom taken time to pause and reflect on my own life, and I was surprised by my own realizations now. The radio blasted Beyoncé's "Run the World (Girls)," and I turned up the volume while trying to gather my thoughts. It all had happened so fast, as if somebody had lifted me with a big set of tongs and shaken me. Of course I would feel dizzy when I was finally put down again, but maybe it wasn't such a bad thing. It had obviously made me calmer and had given me more perspective than I'd had before. I felt grateful for seeing things more clearly now, even though a person shouldn't have to receive a cancer diagnosis before starting to think about what is important in life. *Well*, I thought, getting a steadier grip around the steering wheel, *better late than never*.

I slowed down before a sharp curve and decided to try to keep to the speed limit. I knew there was a school ahead, and I didn't want to cause any problems. My thoughts wandered to a headline I had seen the other day in the newspaper. A man on his way to work had hit a mom and her kid in the morning traffic. They had died later that day. The tragic memory made me gasp for air.

It struck me that my case wasn't unique. Life can change in a heartbeat for everyone, so the best thing we can do is to value what we have while we still have it.

The thought gave me chills, and I decided to turn back home.

CHAPTER 20

Mia came for a visit every afternoon. I would take a nap to have enough energy to spend time with her, and we would sit on the couches out on the porch. It felt a bit weird to hang out; it was just like when we were kids, only we weren't.

One day we were having tea, even though I preferred coffee. All the medications had messed up my stomach, and I had to be gentle with it. We sat in silence and looked at my parents' garden, where we had spent so much time when we were kids. Dad was busy mowing the lawn, and I inhaled the scent of newly cut grass. I liked it, and the buzzing sound of the mower in the background made me calm.

We were browsing through the old school yearbook, laughing about our choices of clothes and hairstyles. We went through all of our classmates and updated each other about what had happened. There was Emil, who always picked his nose when he thought nobody could see; the beautiful Natasha, who was popular among the boys; and the unforgettable Alice, who was always late even though she lived two minutes away.

"Look! There's Carl with the curly hair. Didn't you used to have a crush on him?" Mia's eyes glowed when I immediately turned the page.

"That was then. Let's look at the other classes!"

I did my best to act cool, but I could tell she was amused by my sudden change of topic. Surprisingly enough, she let it slide. When we found a picture of her first love, we both burst out in a snorting laugh. When we calmed down, she leaned closer to get a good look at him.

"Oh my God! I remember that long hair—I thought he looked like that guy from the Hanson brothers, but looking at him now I guess I was wrong..."

"Oh, come on, he wasn't that bad."

"Oh, but he was." She tried to keep serious, but instead a grunting sound slipped out, which made her laugh even harder. It was infectious, and I joined in till my stomach almost cramped.

"You know that if you laugh often enough, it's almost like exercise. I read somewhere that you'll get abs that way."

"Really?"

She winked at me. "Of course."

It made me think of something, and I put the yearbook down. "I can't keep you here until I get well—you know that, right?"

"Look, I will stay a few days to begin with, and then we'll see. Don't worry about that now, let's make sure we make the most out of the time we have instead."

She had the right approach, and I squeezed her hand. "You know, when I studied at the university, we had exchange students from all over the world in some of the classes. I remember that I thought that there was no use in getting close to them since they were going home when the semester was over. I believe it has something to do with our culture and that we are not keen to invest in something that is not long term. However, a dear friend of mine who was born in the Middle East had a totally different view. He said that if a group of people are here only for a short while, it's even more important that you get to know them quickly, so that you can spend as much time as possible together before separation. That's how you and I should act now."

"Exactly! He sounds like a wise friend to me," she said and leaned her head back. We sat there in silence for a while, both caught up in our own thoughts. Then she turned to me and opened her mouth as if to say something but then closed it again.

"What is it?" Her hesitation caught my interest; her mouth was usually like an unstoppable machine gun.

"What more has changed since the operation? I mean, do you view everything differently now than before the diagnosis?"

Her question raised so many thoughts, and they swirled around like a hurricane, increasing in strength by the minute. I did my best to separate them, but if I pulled one out, another one was created. She must have noticed my internal struggle, because she put her hand on mine. I looked at her with a troubled face.

"I don't even know where to start."

"I've got time. Only if you want to share, though."

"Well, actually I want to talk about it. What is the point of this happening if I don't learn from it? I never had this much time before to really think about what I want and who I am. For a start, the illness has forced me to take it slower and to be in the moment. I've never done so few things a day as now, and that is frustrating, but on the other hand, I have the time to enjoy everything I do. Before, when I tried to squeeze the most possible out of every day, my life was like a dry dishcloth."

"That sounds tiresome. But at least you lived every day to the fullest."

"No, that's the thing. I didn't. From an outside perspective, maybe, but I did everything halfhearted; I wasn't present. I did so many things, I couldn't enjoy any of it. I was on the verge of breaking in the middle."

"Why did you do it, then?" She made it sound so simple.

I was silent for a long while. "I believe it was fear of missing out."

I breathed out and all of a sudden felt tired. For the first time, I realized that fear was the cause.

"To me it sounds like you put too much pressure on yourself." Mia had a troubled wrinkle between her eyes.

"Well . . . I saw tiredness as a sign of weakness." It struck me that I would never say these words to a friend who complained about being tired, so why had I been so strict with myself?

"You know what you need?" Mia said, and her eyes lit up like when she was a child and had been up to something. She must have seen that I had no clue, because she didn't wait for my response before she exclaimed, "Yoga!"

Oh no, I was afraid she would suggest something like that. My mind went to a movie I had seen a while back. It was about a man who got fed up with his life and went to India to meditate and practice yoga. It was too clichéd and way too spiritual for my taste.

"Eh . . . or we can just go shopping?" I said and winked at her.

"Don't try, missy, you should at least give it a chance!" She reached for her phone and started to search for something. When she looked up, her eyes sparkled. "They have started a yoga center in town!" She scrolled down a bit and then exclaimed that they had a class the next day. "Let's go!" When I didn't answer right away she looked at me with big eyes and pouting lips. She reminded me of a kid trying to convince her parents to let her go to the amusement park. When she batted her eyelids I sighed and finally gave in.

"All right, I'll give it a try."

"Great! I think you'll love it!"

I wasn't so sure, but I knew she wouldn't stop trying to convince me once she had an idea. I was getting tired, and I think she noticed, because she grabbed her sweater and kissed me on the cheek.

"See you tomorrow, then. I'll come pick you up at four p.m."

"Can't wait," I muttered and followed her to the front door.

CHAPTER 21

I looked through my old wardrobe for workout clothes without any hope of finding anything. I had barely any things left at my parents' place, or so I thought. To my surprise I found an old T-shirt and jogging pants. They would have to do. I had always viewed yoga as a useless workout, since you didn't leave the training sweaty. When you were pressed for time, half an hour on the treadmill gave better results; you could see your progress, and the calories disappear. Now I had almost too much time on my hands, so I guessed it couldn't hurt to try. After all, Mia had seemed so keen on bringing me.

The doorbell rang, and I grabbed a sweater and headed out.

We arrived five minutes early. That gave us time to rent yoga mats and familiarize ourselves with the small room. It was warm and had a slightly sweet scent of incense. There were already a few people there, and we put our mats in the back. I looked around. The brick walls were decorated with fabrics in different beige colors, and on some of them a Buddha was painted. The lady in front of me had started to do the splits while waiting for the class to begin. I was stiff as a tree trunk and couldn't have felt more out of place. I rolled my eyes at Mia but tried to focus when the instructor came in and closed the door. He was tall and skinny, and his long black hair was in a ponytail. I wondered if he was one of those people who fasted every now and then—with his bones sticking out under his stretched skin, he sure looked like he didn't get enough to eat.

Halfway through the class, I started to get annoyed. We bent our bodies in ways I had never done before, and the instructor kept reminding us to breathe. The lady in front of me seemed to have no problem bending in any direction, as if her spine were made out of jelly. I tried to do the same movements as her, but they only resulted in my back cracking, and for a moment I thought I'd broken something. It felt like we stretched for an hour, and I wondered if I would get the least sweaty. This was definitely different from the intense workouts I was used to.

After what felt like an eternity, the instructor said, "Namaste," and declared the session over. He suggested we stay for a voluntary relaxation exercise, and I looked at Mia and hoped she would skip it. To my dismay she smiled and sat down again, and I could not do much other than join, too. The instructor asked us to lie down and handed us blankets to keep us warm. He started talking in a softer way, asking us to thank our bodies for letting us exercise. He continued to talk about how body and soul were connected, and how true well-being comes when we have a balance between the two. At first I didn't pay any attention, but when I started to listen to what he was saying, it actually made sense.

***

"So what did you think?" Mia backed up the car and looked at me, her eyes filled with expectation.

"Well . . . it's not really my cup of tea. But I have to admit I'm feeling more relaxed now."

"Told you so." She seemed happy enough and turned the car around in the parking lot.

"The guy looked ascetic, though. Do you think we should bring him an ice cream next time?"

She laughed and nodded her head. "Yeah, he is thin. But so strong, didn't you notice?" she said with a steady grip on the wheel.

"I guess." I remembered the headstand he had done without any problems at the end. I looked out the window. The relaxation session had made me think. I had never thought of health the way the instructor described it. My image of a healthy person was someone who hit the gym regularly and didn't eat fast food, but maybe I had been wrong. The instructor had stressed the importance of having a balanced lifestyle. Maybe it was as important to prioritize sleep and time to do nothing as it was to be physically active.

"What are you thinking about?" Mia's voice brought me back to reality again.

"Oh, nothing . . . it's just, I might have underestimated relaxation."

She didn't say anything, and it was like she expected me to continue.

"I mean, it feels like I'm always hunting for something. I even walk fast when I'm not in a hurry!"

She laughed. "Yep, you have always been a bit hyperactive."

"Yeah, I've never really seen the benefit of taking it easy. But maybe it's good to plan some time in the calendar to do nothing, like the instructor said. That way you get time to ask yourself where you are going, and if you are on the right track." I scratched my head. The wig was itching.

"Yep, that's what they say." Mia was focused on the road, and I went back to my own thoughts. Where was I going? To be honest, I didn't know, but at least I had asked the question for the first time in twenty-eight years. I hoped that would count for something.

CHAPTER 22

"Are you happy?" The question was straightforward and sounded almost harsh. I knew Mia didn't mean anything negative or sarcastic by it; she was genuinely interested. We sat in her parents' kitchen. We'd both felt we needed a change of scenery, but neither of us had the energy to go all the way to town. Our coffee meet-ups had become a habit by then, and we always got into philosophical discussions sooner or later. I guessed that she didn't have the patience for small talk that day.

I turned the question around. "Are you?"

"Hey! Don't try, missy. I asked you first." She gave me a sly look.

I rolled my eyes and let her have her way. Some things were not worth fighting over. "OK, OK. But God . . . what a complicated question."

"Not really," Mia said quickly. "I mean, it is hard to answer since we are not used to getting the question straight up like this, but it can still be answered with yes or no."

"Mm, I guess you are right." I thought for a bit about what had happened recently, and with that in mind I guess the answer should have been quite obvious. There was a thought in the back of my mind that cried for attention, though, and it stopped me from answering. I acknowledged the idea, and rolled it around two or three times before I decided to spit it out.

"You know what is quite alarming?" I didn't wait for her answer; instead, I continued. "I believe I am. I am at least happier now than before I knew I was ill."

"Really?" She sounded as surprised as I felt.

"Yeah . . ." I knew I had to elaborate; she was stubborn, and she wouldn't stop asking until I gave her a satisfying answer.

"It is hard to pinpoint exactly what it is. It's many things that have changed. I believe the biggest aspect, though, is that I'm more grateful now than before the diagnosis." I reached for a glass of water next to my cup of coffee. All this talking made my throat dry.

"You know the feeling when you lose something? Let's say, for example, you have an old and quite shitty car that you hate. Well, imagine that car breaks down, and it takes a week for it to be repaired. In the meantime, you are forced to take the metro or bus instead. All of a sudden you share the space with a large number of people who are stressed, tired, and annoyed. You might not get a seat, and the air will be filled with sweat and frustration. On top of that, the person next to you might have really bad breath and refuse to stop talking to you. After a week, you will be so relieved and grateful for your shitty little car. It will change from being something to be embarrassed about to being representative of a huge freedom."

"That's true!" Mia leaned forward. "That's exactly how I feel when I have a slight fever. I feel so utterly bad for myself, and I promise myself to be grateful for my health when I get better. It's just that . . . then I get better, and it takes two days till I have forgotten about it. Old habits die hard."

I gave her a smile of recognition. "I'm exactly the same. That's why we need to remind ourselves every day. Lately, before I go to bed, I make a list in my mind of at least three things that happened during the day that I'm grateful for. I read about this technique somewhere, and I'm telling you, it really works!"

Mia's eagerness turned into skepticism. Her body language betrayed her; she leaned back in her chair, and I could tell she thought I was talking about fluffy things.

"It doesn't work all the time. What if it is a really shitty day . . . and you don't have anything to be grateful for?"

"Well, I can't say I don't have my dark moments, I do. But no matter what happens, there is always something good to hold on to. I mean, if by the end of the day you are able to give a friend a hug, then it's still an OK day." I recalled the last day I was really down, and it gave me the chills. It wasn't easy, that's for sure.

I paused and let the words sink in for both of us. I could almost hear how her brain twisted, turning my statements around in her mind and trying to decide if they were useful or not. Her forehead had three deep wrinkles, but after a while they turned to only one, and I prepared myself for a new question. She tilted her head and raised an eyebrow while looking at me. "What is it that you lost?"

"Excuse me?" That was not what I expected her to say. Now it was her turn to explain.

"You said that to be truly grateful, you need to know how it feels to lose something."

I took a deep breath before I answered. "You misunderstood me. I haven't lost anything—yet. I'm aware of the statistics regarding my cancer type. On average, people live only a few years after diagnosis. So in a way it's much easier for me to appreciate the small things every day, since I know for a fact that I won't have them forever. But I'm confident that anyone, illness or not, is able to appreciate everyday life and live every day to the fullest. It's a matter of practicing with your mind." I felt my heart pumping faster; this was such an important topic, and I couldn't stay neutral.

"Got ya—I'll start with the list of three things tonight."

"Good. I think you'll notice a difference," I said joyfully and reached for a cookie. Mia reached for one, too, and started to eat it in that funny way she used to do when we were kids. Instead of taking a normal bite, she peeled off the top layer and put it on her plate. She ate the filling and the bottom layer, where the most chocolate was, and then left the rest. I glanced at her plate, and when she realized it, she smiled and offered me the last piece.

I couldn't help but wonder if this was why we got on so well—we completed each other like night and day.

I ate the piece she gave me in one go then let out a big sigh, and Mia smiled at me.

"Time to call it a day?"

I felt a bit embarrassed that I didn't have more energy. "I'm like a granny," I joked, but she just shook her head.

"Come on. The most good-looking granny I've seen, in that case." She winked at me.

***

After she dropped me off at home, I went into my old room to have a nap. Before I fell asleep, I went over what we had discussed. It was pretty weird, actually, that I considered myself happier now than before the illness, especially since the only thing I had changed was my state of mind. *The brain is a powerful tool*, I thought, which was a bit ironic considering where my tumor was located. Of course, I sometimes wished none of this had happened, that I didn't have to go through it, but on the other hand, I doubted that I would have ever changed the stressful way I lived if it hadn't been for the big punch in the face the cancer monster had given me. Sometimes we need to be shaken up, and then it's up to ourselves how we choose to react.

CHAPTER 23

The next day Mia came to our house earlier than usual. It was sunny outside, so we decided to go out on the porch. I was making myself comfortable on one of the sofas when she reached for something in her bag. She had a curious smile on her lips and handed me a box filled with heart-shaped chocolate pralines.

"We need to get in the right mood," she said with a laugh.

"For what?"

"You haven't told me about the guys." She sat down on the other sofa opposite me.

I let out a small laugh. "What guys?" My love life stood pretty still at the moment, and I had no intention of changing that. What would I have said on a date? "Hey, I'm on long-term sick leave, but it's not something serious. Or, wait, it is."

"Oh, I'm sure you have some gossip I haven't heard," she said and looked at me like a kid who was up to something.

I bit my lip. Was she aiming at Carl, whom I had been in love with since third grade? I gave her a gaze that could kill, but she only laughed, blew a kiss my way, and lay down to make herself more comfortable. I studied the sofa and wished my parents had changed the hideous cover. With its brown-and-orange floral pattern, it looked like it belonged in a seventies movie.

Mia lay on one side with her head in her hand, and the wrinkle between her eyes was back again. She chewed on the inside of her cheek, and I knew what that meant. A question was coming up.

"How do you feel about dating when you know you're probably not gonna live till you are a hundred years old?"

A wave of fear hit me, and I had to shake it off before I could continue. "Whoa, what kind of question is that?"

I had forgotten how direct Mia could be and wished for a moment I could get up and leave—she was hitting too close to what I had been worrying about.

"I'm sorry. Do you love me anyway?" Her eyes grew bigger until she reminded me of a cute puppy. She pouted and didn't stop blinking until she had me laughing.

"That's actually interesting," I said when I had caught my breath, and I sat up straighter. "I had always had a hard time saying those three little words. We seldom used them at our house, and you're the only friend I've said them to. Do you remember how we used to practice together? We couldn't get the words out at first, but after some practice it wasn't so scary anymore."

She burst into laughter and accidentally let out a loud grunt, which had become her signature laugh by then.

"Of course I remember! God, who would have thought it would be that hard—and it's supposed to be something natural, right? Do you think it's a cultural thing?"

"Mm, maybe. Or it's just different in different families. As a kid you watch behaviors, then mimic them. So if nobody in your house showed their love in an outspoken way, I guess it's hard to get used to. My parents never said it to each other, for example. It doesn't mean they didn't love each other; they just didn't put it into words."

"Sounds like my family . . ." She became silent.

"That's one thing I have changed since the diagnosis."

"What?" She came back to reality again and turned her head to see me better.

"I'm sure I'm not the same person now as before the diagnosis, but I have a hard time pinpointing exactly what has changed. But this is definitely one of them. Nowadays I tell people that I hold dear how much they mean to me, as soon as it pops up in my head. I see no reason not to, and I don't want to disappear from this planet without people knowing how I feel. They shouldn't have to wonder what I think about them, they should just know."

"That's nice." Mia sat up and reached for the box of candy. She seemed to be paying more attention to choosing a chocolate praline than to what I had just said.

I decided to try a different explanation. "Just imagine lying on your deathbed knowing that your siblings don't know how much you love them. We should tell the ones we love every single day. We're good at telling our partner that we love him or her, but what about the rest of the people around us?"

"Are you following your own advice?" Mia seemed restless and sat up and pulled her knees up to her chin, putting her arms around her legs like she needed protection.

"I think so . . . even though there is one person I never told how I felt."

"Let me guess . . . Carl, is it?" Her eyes lit up. "I knew it!" When I didn't object, she did a small dance of triumph with her arms.

"I didn't realize how much you liked him."

"Yeah, I hid it pretty well," I said. "I was too shy back then." I had my chances to tell him how I felt a few times, though,

I reminded myself. I'd run into him on a business trip in Stockholm about a year earlier. I smiled at the memory. He was now living in the capital of Sweden and worked in one of the big banks. From what I could tell, he was doing well. Not much had changed, though; he looked handsome as always, and it was ridiculous how I still got red cheeks when I met up with him, even years later. How could I ever tell him how I felt? He was the popular kid in school, and I was . . . well, ordinary.

"You should tell him before it's too late." Mia's words brought me back from my thoughts.

"I know, but I keep on postponing it. And now I'm not in Stockholm anyway . . ." I said slowly.

"I hear the voice of somebody who is avoiding her own life lesson." Mia gave me a provocative smile and a friendly nudge.

"OK, I promise I'll do it, OK? I just need to get better first."

"Fair enough. But I'll remind you, that's for sure."

I knew she would, and just the thought of it made me almost nauseated. I decided that the best I could do was to change the topic.

"I almost forgot, I wanted to show you something." I got up a bit too fast to get my tablet and heard my own voice increasing in speed, telling her about a dress I had seen online. It was obvious I had escaped the subject, but it seemed like she would let me get away with it.

Soon we were absorbed by H&M's new collection, and the old-flame discussion faded away.

Apparently love was a sensitive subject that we might get back to later, but for now I was happy just to sit next to my best friend, joking around like old times.

CHAPTER 24

Even though I decided to tackle the situation with a positive mind-set, some days were harder than others. On those days, my mind ran away from me and played its own game, and my attempts to tame it didn't always work. I was angry at the world and asked myself pointless questions, such as why, and came back to reasoning that it wasn't fair. I hated those dark moments, but I guess I needed them. Mia played a big part in helping me realize it was OK to be sad and angry for a while, as long as it didn't turn into a permanent state.

It was three p.m., the time she usually arrived for our afternoon coffee. The doorbell rang, but I couldn't make myself get up and open the door. The shrill noise kept on ringing. She knew I was home and started to create an annoying melody with the doorbell until I couldn't take it any longer. Still in my pajamas, I went to open the door and let her in. She studied me from head to toe, and I could see a wrinkle form on her forehead. I knew I must look like shit, as I had not left the bed the whole day, or showered or eaten anything since the day before. It was as if the tears I didn't let out had formed a big cloud inside me, and there was no room for food. I quickly went back to bed and pulled the duvet up to my chin while Mia took off her shoes in the hallway. A minute later she popped her head into the dark bedroom. I barely looked at her. I wasn't trying to be rude, I was just dead tired, even though I had slept all day. She didn't wait for a cue to come in, she just walked straight to the window and pulled the curtains aside. The light hurt my eyes, and I pulled the duvet over my head. She opened the window to let in some fresh air, then walked over and sat next to me in bed.

"OK, missy, what's wrong?"

At first I didn't reply and hoped that my silence would scare her away. I should have known better. Mia wasn't one to back down.

"Look, I get if you don't want to talk about it. But it usually helps, and you know it."

I let out a deep sigh. Why did she always have to be right? She pulled the duvet away so she could look me in the eyes. I blinked like I had never seen the light before. She didn't take her eyes off me until I gave up and pulled myself to an almost upright position.

We didn't talk at first, as I was too busy trying to find words for what I felt. She seemed happy to have woken me up from my trance and didn't seem to be in a hurry.

"I'm just so . . . angry." Not a very vivid explanation, but it was what my tired brain could come up with at the moment.

I could see on her face that she was surprised by the hopelessness in my voice. It was quite cute, actually; her right eyebrow always raised a bit more than the left. "Finally! I thought you would never say it—you're always so positive."

"I know . . . I guess everyone has bad days now and then." My voice was weaker than usual, and I reached for the glass of water next to the bed. She helped me put another pillow behind my back to get on her level.

"What are you angry about?" She looked at me with her big green eyes, clearly caught a bit off guard with my choice of topic for the day.

"You know, I didn't realize it until yesterday when I was talking to my mom. First I thought I was sad, but now I know that I'm frustrated. I feel like punching somebody." I saw her face get stiff and added, "Don't worry—not you." I sighed deeply. "I'm being positive ninety percent of the time, but sometimes, especially when I read about my disease, I get so down."

She gave me a strict look, one that reminded me of my old piano teacher when she found out I hadn't practiced.

"You shouldn't read those articles online. We've talked about this!"

"I know, I know." I had wanted to inform myself, but it had backfired big time.

"They are not always right. Statistics are misleading, remember?" Her face was slightly red, and she seemed frustrated. Normally I knew all of this; it was pretty obvious that statistics derived from a test group of people considerably older than myself might not apply to my case, but it didn't matter. I couldn't close my eyes to the fact that it didn't look good.

"Can we just agree that it's a shitty situation and then move on?" She made it sound so simple.

I raised my voice. "It's a fucked-up situation, that's what it is. Think about it—I'm feeding myself poison . . . I'm killing my own cells voluntarily."

"You can't think about your treatment like that, though; it will make you mad. When you look back in six months you will be happy you went through it, and after this nothing can stop you."

"Yeah, I know," I said slowly and got caught in my own thoughts for a while. Mia started to bite her cuticles.

After a few minutes of silence, I realized what was bothering me. Finally, I found the right words to describe my bad mood. "You know what it feels like?"

She shook her head and abandoned her nails for a second.

"I feel like somebody stole my life. With no warning, no nothing. From one day to another, it was gone. Everything I've been fighting for has been put on pause. My colleagues are advancing in their careers, my friends are traveling and seeing new places, meeting new people. And here I am, hairless and clueless about the future."

"Hey—you need to stop those thoughts!" Mia's voice was loud now, almost shrill. It reminded me of the first day we met, when I'd put my chair on top of her new jacket. "Who are you and what have you done with my friend? I have never seen you this bitter before."

I shook my head and looked down. "I know, I know. You're right, I need to lose the attitude. It's just that . . . it's like I'm on a fast-moving train, and it's stopping at all these exciting stations. I see my friends have already gotten off and I'm trying to go with them, but I can't. I see how happy they seem, and I really want to go. I'm telling the conductor to let me off, but he blocks the way."

She looked at me, and a tear slid down her cheek. She leaned over to take my hand, but I pulled it away.

"I'm not saying that you should feel sorry for me. I mean, these things happen. Life happens. I know that I will learn so much from this experience and that I probably will become a better person out of it. But right now"—I looked at her—"I'm just so angry. I want to hold somebody responsible, I want to take action. But the worst part of it is that there is no one. I can't even blame myself."

"What do you mean?" She reached for her purse, which was lying on the floor, and took out a handkerchief.

"One thing I asked the surgeon was if I had lived my life wrong. Had I been drinking too much, eating poorly, or maybe exercising too little?"

"What did he say?"

"Nothing. Imagine that. Nothing. He said that it was pure bad luck." I let out a bitter laugh. "So here I am, angry as hell, but there's nobody to blame. It's out of my control and I hate it."

"If it makes you feel better . . . I believe everybody will meet an evil conductor in their life. Probably not as evil as yours," Mia said with a crooked smile. "But nonetheless, they will have some form of struggle, and sometimes no matter what they do—be it trying to convince the conductor with words or moving him in a more physical way—some things we just can't control." She took a deep breath and thought for a while. "I believe the best thing to do is to try to find out if there is anything you can do to change the situation, and if not, make the most out of it."

I was quiet for a while. Then I smiled a little for the first time that day. "Listen to you—here I am trying to teach you things, and all of a sudden it's the other way around."

She gave me a warm smile, and her dimples were back. "That's what friends are for, isn't it?"

"I just can't lose the feeling that I'm missing out. I see the months passing by, and even if I'm happy for all my friends when they get promoted, I can't help but feel like I'm not developing at all."

"Well, what would you say if somebody took a year off to travel? Maybe even quit their job?"

"Well, that's not the same, they get new experiences out of it."

Her eyebrows rose. "And you don't?"

"I . . . well, I guess I haven't thought of it that way before."

"You need two things. One is patience, and I know that one is difficult for you—you have always liked doing ten things at once."

"What's the second thing?"

Her eyes turned mischievous, as they'd done when we were younger and she was up to something that she knew our parents wouldn't approve of. "I know you're tired. But do you think you'd manage to go for a short ride in the car? I have my parents' car with me."

"What did you have in mind?" I tried to sound indifferent, but we both knew she had caught my interest.

"You'll see."

She helped me get ready, and I thanked my lucky stars that my mom was at work, otherwise she would have talked us out of it. Mia gave me her arm as support as we walked toward the car.

She drove carefully, and I enjoyed the breeze from the open windows. I knew I should be careful about not getting a cold, but at the same time it felt good not to care about all exhortations, just for once. Mia pulled up at the parking lot in front of the military base not far from our house. It was one of the few left in Sweden—we could not exactly brag about the size of our military. They trained young men and women there, which is why we sometimes heard gunshots in the distance. When they didn't practice, it was a great place to walk a dog or go for a run, as the nature was beautiful out there. Every other Sunday, a bunch of guys dressed in green military clothes would fill up the bus from our little village to the base. I guess they all had been on leave, their only chance to get out in public. When we were younger, we loved those Sundays. The guys were not boys, like our childish classmates, and as a fourteen-year-old there was nothing more exciting than trying to get their attention. A sudden gloom spread over my face when I thought about it; it would have been a good memory if not for the fact that it was the same year Mia moved away.

"You OK?" She turned off the engine and looked at me. I forced myself back to reality.

"Yeah, let's go."

We got out, and she locked the door and gave me her arm to hold on to. Together we started walking across the grass toward the running trail. The fresh air was amazing, and I tried to take the deepest breaths possible, so as not to waste any. We had to walk carefully not to step into any rabbit holes, but it suited me just fine after not having worked out in so long. As we got closer to the trail Mia stopped and looked around. There was no one in sight. "Let's do it here."

"Do what?"

"Let your anger out."

When I didn't show any signs of understanding, she cleared her throat. "I find the best thing to do is to scream real loud."

"Are you serious?" I almost started laughing.

"Of course. It will make you feel better. You should be happy I didn't take you to boxing class."

"Well, I wouldn't have been able to punch anyone, so . . ."

"So this is a perfect alternative! Come on, I'll start." She leaned her head back, cleared her throat, and gave out a powerful shriek. The sound gave me goose bumps and reminded me of an old movie I'd seen recently, in which a mother lost her child to slavery. Mia's scream was filled with suppressed anger and frustration. I resisted an urge to cover my ears and looked at her in surprise. How on earth did that small body create such a big sound? And where did all those emotions come from?

"Oh, that felt good. Try it."

Something was holding me back. I couldn't remember the last time I had actually screamed—maybe it was when I used to call our dog, but I wasn't sure that counted. Mia stood in silence next to me, waiting. I thought of the negative doctors I had met, the fact that I might not live through this, that I might never be able to find true love. It wasn't until I realized that I might never become a mother that something released inside of me, and I started crying. Mia let out another long scream, this one even louder than before. I joined in, and together we stood there, in the middle of the empty field, letting all our sorrows and frustrations go. When my voice couldn't bear it any longer, I sank down to the ground, sitting on my heels. The tears were still pouring down silently, like they would never stop, and my nose had started to run. Mia sat down, too, and gave me a big hug that almost caused us to fall over. I don't know how long we sat there. It was like my feelings had disappeared with the screams . . . except for one. I didn't recognize it at first, and even though I tried to put words to it, the closest I could get was a strange emptiness that filled every corner of my body.

Time and space disappeared, and at one point my feet fell asleep.

"Come, let's not get you too tired," Mia whispered softly in my hair. Side by side we walked toward the car, her arm still placed around my shoulders.

On the way back I felt relieved. Maybe it was OK to be sad sometimes. I knew it wouldn't make me look strong, but it would make me human. I was still happy nobody had been there except for us. Glancing over at Mia, I couldn't help being impressed. When did she become this wise? She sure knew what I needed, even before I did.

Back in the car we didn't say much at first, both caught up in our own minds. One thought kept worrying me even though I tried to push it away. If I let it go, I knew it would haunt me, so I decided to confront her.

"What is it that you're not telling me?"

The sudden question seemed to startle her, and she blinked a bit too long before answering. "What do you mean"?

"Nobody screams like that for no reason. What is it you're angry about?"

She shrugged her shoulders, put in the car keys, and started to turn the car around in the parking lot. When she was out on the road, she gave me a quick glance. "You're being neurotic. It's nothing." But the nothing she was talking about was definitely something. I could read her like an open book, and the fact remained: she was hiding something. A cold feeling hit me. Was this connected with why she left all those years ago?

"All along we've been talking only about me. It's time you tell me what's bothering you."

Her grip around the steering wheel tightened, and she stared with empty eyes on the road ahead. She knew I wouldn't let it go, and I could see how she fought with her own thoughts.

"You were the one telling me to let it all out."

A tear started to form in the corner of her eye, and her body got tense, like she was preparing for a fight. Then she must have suddenly changed her mind, as she drove the car to the side of the road and stopped. She leaned back and looked at me with sad eyes. She opened her mouth and closed it again several times before she started to tell me. It was fourteen years later, and I had started to wonder if she would ever open up. Knowing what I knew now, I'm not sure I would have pushed her this way. As her story unfolded, my hands opened and closed in anger, and my throat got tighter. For every word she added, I got closer to tears, and when she finished, my cheeks were completely wet. I tried to keep calm, but my heavy breathing through my nose revealed how furious I was.

"So . . . that's why you left."

"I'm sorry I didn't tell you before. I wanted to . . ."

I put my hand on hers. "You don't have to explain."

"I want to, though. At first I didn't tell anyone, and I guess I got more and more silent. My mom thought it was because of the move and that it would pass, but when I stopped eating, she sent me to a shrink."

"Did it help?"

"Well, I didn't tell her what happened. The first time I spoke about it was a year ago when I started seeing a shrink again." She paused, and I tried to take in what she had just told me. How could she have lived with this secret for so many years?

"I don't understand my own reaction back then, but I think I wanted to shut everything from my old life behind not to get reminded. I guess it was my way of coping, and to pretend it never happened."

I leaned over and hugged her hard. It must have been a weird sight; two women sitting in silence in a car by the side of the road, lost in thought. I didn't care. All I could think about was how to help my best friend, and after a while a plan started to form in my mind.

PART 3

CHAPTER 25

Sweden, August 2001

"Ouch!" Mia had just managed to poke herself in the eye with the mascara brush, and now her eyes were tearing up, resulting in black stripes all over her eyelids. She studied herself in the mirror. This did not look at all like the smoky eyes she had aimed for. Damn it! All that time reading magazine articles didn't seem to have paid off. She opened the bathroom cabinet, found the makeup remover, and prepared herself to start all over again. If only Anna could have been here to ease the tension! Anna had gone away over the weekend to celebrate her grandma's birthday, which meant she would miss the party of the year. The very first party without parents that they had been invited to, and they both agreed that the timing couldn't have been worse. Mia had promised to go anyway and to tell Anna all about it the following Monday. Now she was a bit nervous, though—she had always had Anna by her side, and to show up alone felt a bit scary. She hesitated for a second, but then decided that she would look like a coward if she didn't go, and she gripped the makeup brush more steadily. How silly she was! She was supposed to be excited; none of the others from her class had been invited. All the girls her age would have killed for this opportunity. There would be older boys and probably alcohol. She knew she would never have been invited if not for the fact that her cousin was arranging the party. His parents were away for the weekend, and he had told them he would take good care of the house. This was her chance to show him she wasn't a little girl anymore! She turned around and pulled out a green dress from her closet. It went well with her light red hair, and she did a few dance moves before looking for a cardigan to go with it. It was summer, but the evenings could get pretty chilly.

She stepped on something, and when she bent down she saw it was a photo of her and Anna from when they were kids. Anna had her blond hair in a ponytail, and her round glasses made her look like a real bookworm. Mia couldn't help smiling—it wasn't like she looked any cooler, with her shiny braces and red fringe. She smiled at the picture and started to tear up, but this time it wasn't the mascara's fault. She still had not gotten used to the thought of moving. It would be bad enough to move to another city, and now her parents had decided to move to another country! She had not spoken to them since they'd dropped the bomb two days ago, and she was determined to keep the icy facade till they reconsidered. Anna had been devastated when she'd told her, and together they agreed that if Mia just showed her parents how upset she was, they would have to change their minds sooner or later. Mia wiped a tear and decided to pull herself together—she couldn't show up all red and swollen to her first party.

**

A few hours later, Mia found herself in the hallway of her aunt's house. The music was loud, and there were people everywhere. It was so crowded, she could barely make her way to the kitchen, and everywhere she looked there were unfamiliar faces. She didn't recognize anyone and decided to look for her cousin. She found him by the kitchen counter, busy mixing drinks. He lit up when he saw her.

"Hey, you made it!"

"Yeah, my parents think I'm at a friend's place for a sleepover."

"Ha-ha, right on!" His red hair moved up and down when he laughed, and he handed her a plastic cup with something dark in it.

"Try it, and tell me it's not the best rum and Coke you've ever had."

She didn't want to admit that this was the very first time she had tried alcohol, so she took a sip and gave him a thumbs-up. The drink was too sweet for her taste but made her warm inside, so she kept drinking it. She looked around. Who were all these people? She felt small and wondered if everybody knew she was younger. As always, she didn't want to show her insecurity, and she tried her best to blend in among the new faces. A guy who was a head taller bumped into her, and when he apologized, she could feel his beer breath. He was quite cute with his curly hair, and she didn't protest when he used her shoulder to recover his balance.

"Mattias," he shouted in her ear.

"Nice to meet you, I'm Mia," she shouted back, and when he smiled at her, she could see that his pupils were enormous. He seemed friendly, though, and told her to join him and his friends in the living room. He took her hand and dragged her through the crowd. She took a deep breath and tried not to spill her drink on the way. *Fake it till you make it,* she thought and took another sip.

A few hours later, everything was spinning. At first she liked the feeling—it made her say things she usually didn't, and she couldn't remember when she had laughed so hard before. Everything seemed funny! Mattias and his friends were all smoking something that had a sweet smell, and they were so easy to talk to. It was like she had known them for a long time, and they all thought it was so cool that she might move to Austria.

"We'll come and visit you!" Mattias shouted, and the others agreed it was a great idea.

"Yeah, let's do it, man!" A guy in a Nirvana T-shirt with long hair blew out some smoke and seemed excited.

"Awesome." A girl with pink hair squeezed down in the sofa next to Mia and hugged her. "We'll become best friends!"

It was all a bit much, seeing that she had just met these people, and Mia excused herself to go to the bathroom. When she stood up, her head started to spin even faster, and she had to hold on to the sofa not to fall. She made her way toward what she thought was the bathroom, closed the door, and sank down to the floor. How nice it was to sit on the cold floor! There wasn't much space, but she could at least put her legs out and lean her head against the door. The music wasn't as loud in there, and she closed her eyes for a second. She wanted to go home and make popcorn with Anna. Why did she have to be away this weekend? She couldn't remember anymore and felt annoyed. Just as she started to relax, someone opened the door. It came as a surprise, and she tumbled out, finding herself lying on the floor and looking up at her cousin. She started to giggle, but he pulled her up and asked if she was hurt.

"What are you doing in the closet anyway?" It was a valid question, but she couldn't think of a good answer. She felt a sudden wave of nausea and looked around for the bathroom. When she saw it, she almost fell trying to reach it as fast as possible. Her cousin wasn't far behind, and when she started to sob in the sink, he closed the door.

"That's it, you need to go home."

It felt like a punch in the stomach, and she lifted her head in protest, only to feel the dizziness come back. She put her head down and vomited into the sink for what felt like forever. He held back her hair while cursing that he'd ever invited her.

She sulked and repeated how sorry she was, until he said it was OK and helped her out into the hallway. He got her a glass of water, and when she felt better she stood up slowly, determined to leave with her head held high.

"Are you sure you can get home by yourself?"

"It's like five minutes away." She had already shamed herself in front of all his friends, and the last thing she wanted was to cause him any more trouble. "It's fine, I'm sure."

He walked her out, and she could feel his eyes on her back as she stumbled over the lawn toward the gate. She pulled the cardigan closer and squinted to see in the pitch-dark. She longed for her bed and promised herself she wouldn't do this again. She started walking down the road but had to stop after only a few minutes. Her head wouldn't stop spinning, and she paused for a moment to regain her balance. As she stilled herself, she heard a crunching noise, like someone was walking toward her. She peered behind her and saw that she was right, a tall shadow was making its way toward her. She recognized the silhouette and froze. Trying to breathe as quietly as possible, she didn't dare move. When he was so close she could see his face, she took a step back.

"Well, what are you doing here in the middle of the night? Isn't it past your bedtime?"

Peter looked the same, even though she had not seen him since he had started high school. It had been such a relief when he graduated, but here he was again, taller and more muscular than ever. He grinned at her, and when she thought of it, he looked like a hyena.

"What is it—you're not scared of me, are you?"

"No . . ." She tried to straighten up to look more confident but wasn't too sure how well she managed.

"Look at you, you've grown some boobs!" He took a step forward, and all her confidence blew away. She put her arms across her chest, as if to protect herself. He leaned down and stroked her face with his hand. The bare touch of his fingers made her shiver, and she tried to look for a way to escape. How fast could he be, was it worth trying to outrun him? *Maybe in a sober state*, she thought, and she felt the panic rise inside her. He gripped her chin steadily and pulled her closer. When his lips touched hers, she tried to get loose. She twisted and turned until he released her, and then she looked at him in disgust. He smelled like old beer, and the look in his eyes scared her. They were wide open, and she recognized his way of slowly licking his lips. He was up to something, and she didn't want to stay and find out what. He grabbed her arm hard, and she tried to punch him. His reflexes were good, and her hand barely touched his face, but it was enough to make his eyes wild. He pulled her to the side of the road and into the bushes before he pushed her down onto the ground.

"So you think you can hit me, you little whore?"

She started crying when he sat on top of her and held her arms down.

"Do you know what I do with people like you?"

She turned her head and tried to move to make his grip looser. It didn't work, he just took a firmer grip around her wrists. He leaned over her and whispered in her ear, "I teach them a lesson."

Her eyes widened as he started to undo his belt. She was so scared, she couldn't move or scream. His wild eyes met hers, and the look he gave her would haunt her as long as she could remember.

***

She had never felt so alone before. She pulled her briefs up and rolled over on one side. She knew she should continue home, but what could happen that was worse than this? The tears streamed across her face, and she wagged from side to side, wailing like a hurt kitten. Her lower abdomen hurt like somebody had cut her, and she was cold. She didn't know how long she laid there, but when it started to rain she pulled herself up and limped home.

***

The next day Mia told her parents that she would gladly move to Austria—after all, a change could be good. When Anna came home and asked about the party, Mia couldn't look her in the eyes, so she just answered briefly. She had a terrible feeling inside, being ashamed of what had happened. She didn't tell anyone, and it was almost ironic how well the move suited her sudden need to escape. She told all her classmates that she was sad to leave, but in her mind she had already started to count down the days till she could leave everything behind.

CHAPTER 26
Sweden, 2015

I sat by the kitchen window at my parents' home with a cup of coffee, waiting for Mia to arrive. I bit my lip and felt disgusted when I thought about what she had told me two days earlier. It had been hard for her to tell me the full story, but I was grateful she had. I knew I couldn't make the horrible memory go away, but maybe I could make it easier for her to move on. I had not been able to save her all those years ago, but it was different now, and I desperately wanted to help. I had formed a plan for how this could happen, but when I told Mia her first reaction was that it would never work. She said it was too much of a hassle, but I could tell that her words were based in fear. In my opinion, she had already opened the door to her past again, and I believed my plan would help her close it for good.

We spent hours discussing it, and finally she realized that it was something that needed to be done. She had one condition, though: that I also deal with some unfinished business.

I took a sip of coffee and looked at my black weekend bag on the floor. My feelings were all over the place. Parts of me were excited and parts of me nervous. I was worried, too—the kind of worry that makes you question your decisions and bugs you every five minutes, wondering if what you are about to do is a good idea or not. Well, we had nothing to lose.

We were about to visit some people we should have faced a long time ago, but as many of us do, we had postponed it and told ourselves that the right time would come. It sure had arrived, and there was no turning back now.

***

Mia almost turned her big suitcase over in the hallway because of the weight, and I wondered how it would fit into Mom's small car. It was a Ford Ka and not made for a lot of luggage—but then again, my bag wasn't as big, so I thought we might make it anyway.

"What on earth did you bring? We will only be away a few days."

"You might think it's only a few days . . . but have you checked where these people live? It's likely they have moved—"

"That's why I have you." I cut her off before she could give me another lecture and smiled as she leaned her suitcase against the wall. She had always been a better planner than me; when I got an idea, I wanted to put it into practice right away.

"If I'm doing this, I need names and a computer . . . and some time."

"Oh. I thought we could check it in the car while driving." I pouted in disappointment. I wanted to get on the road as fast as possible, before we changed our mind. "We need to be back for the new round of chemo anyway, and that's in two weeks." The thought gave me chills.

"You better give me a list with names, then," Mia said with her hands on her hips. Short and concise. She would have made a great CEO. I knew at least I would have followed her to the end of the world. I went to get pen and paper, and half an hour later we had a list ready.

***

"I need coffee. And I think we're lost." She took the first exit she could find, and the sudden move forced her to step on the brake pedal. The time it took her to slow down suggested she had been driving well above the speed limit of seventy-five miles per hour. Good thing nobody was behind us. She was a good driver, though, and it didn't take long before she steered us into a small parking lot with a skilled hand. It was nice to get some fresh air, and we both stretched our arms and legs before heading for the main entrance of a small restaurant. It was dark inside, and we quickly ordered a coffee each and went back out in the sunlight again.

We were the only guests and seated ourselves at a wooden table next to a small lawn. It was a beautiful day, and I closed my eyes and leaned back against the chair with my face toward the sun.

Mia was busy checking the driving directions on her phone. "Did they have to move so far?" Her voice sounded annoyed, and she moved around on the bench as though she were itchy. "There's about two hours left." She behaved just as I did before the diagnosis: restless and stressed, creating a deadline for everything even though there was no need for it.

"Well, other than my ass hurting, it's no problem—we're not in a hurry, are we?" I asked. "We need to do this," I reminded her, hoping she had not changed her mind.

She put down the phone and looked at me with sad eyes. "I know, sweetie, I know. Sorry, I'm just a bit carsick."

Almost two and a half hours later we pulled up to the driveway of a small house. It seemed to be a friendly neighborhood, with kids playing in the gardens. A guy was mowing his lawn on the other side of a hedge. I looked at the address on the front door and confirmed that it was number 20. The house was well taken care of; the lawn had been recently cut, and red flowers had been neatly planted beneath the two front windows.

Mia peered at the house, and her whole body froze.

"Maybe this isn't a good idea after all," she said and scratched her arm.

"Maybe not... but I don't think you'll ever be able to move on if you don't face him again."

We sat in silence for quite a while, and it was starting to get awkward when she suddenly broke the silence.

"What if they aren't home?" She had not taken her hands off the steering wheel, as though she were waiting for me to give her permission to turn back.

"Then we'll wait." *We traveled the whole day; he has to be home*, I thought a bit nervously.

A woman with curly blond hair opened the door. She looked like a housewife taken from a magazine from the fifties, wearing an apron decorated with small flowers and with two small kids hanging on to her legs. They looked as surprised as she was to see us, and they all waited for me to explain our mission. A small dog appeared and passed us like it had been hit by lightning. Before any of us had the time to react, the little fuzzy black-and-white creature escaped through the gate and disappeared around the corner.

"Oh shit." Her voice was light and didn't seem to belong to a fragile woman like herself.

"Mommy said a bad word!" The kids started to giggle and went after the dog. They competed over who could run the fastest, and I got worried they would run out onto the road. The apron lady didn't seem worried, though, just annoyed.

"It's a calm area; he won't get far. Now, how can I help you?"

Since Mia seemed to have lost her voice, I stepped in. "We used to know Peter when we were kids."

"Oh, OK . . . my name is Karin. I'm his wife." When we got closer to shake hands, I noticed a bruise that went across her eyebrow and down her right cheek. She had done her best to cover it with makeup, and I didn't want to know how bad it looked without foundation. My fists tightened. Seemed like he had not changed a bit.

"He should be home any minute. Why don't you come in?" She was exactly how I would have imagined his other half to be: polite, submissive, and a bit shy. He probably made all the decisions for both of them, and I was surprised she invited us inside. We came into a narrow hallway that led to the kitchen. It smelled like meat, and I guessed she was preparing dinner. The curtains were made from the same yellow fabric as her apron and revealed her eye for details. We were shown into the living room; it, too, was small, and the sofas matched the cloth on the coffee table. Everything else was in different green shades and looked cozy and inviting. Was I in the right house? Karin prepared tea and made an effort to make small talk a bit.

"Were you close?"

The question made Mia uncomfortable, and she got up to look out the window, holding her arms around herself like protection from something we couldn't see. I stayed put on the sofa. "Not really." I could see that my answer puzzled her, even though she did her best not to show it.

"But you did go to the same school?"

I nodded, and at the same time the door opened and the barking dog was back. Together with the kids, the small fluffy pet tumbled in and messed up the carpet. I heard heavy steps and then a tall man appeared in the doorway.

"You didn't tell me you would have friends over." His voice was harsh and accusing.

Karin stood up, and her posture was defensive. Her back was slightly bent, and she almost looked afraid. "These women said they knew you as a child. I just wanted to be polite."

Peter turned to us, and his jaw dropped. Mia was still staring out the window, pretending like nothing was happening. His eyes wandered between the two of us, as if he couldn't decide whom to approach first. For a moment it was like he had lost all his confidence; he didn't look like the scornful bully I remembered.

He was pale when he finally cleared his throat and told his wife to bring the kids upstairs.

She didn't question him, just did as she was told, and after they'd all left, a strange emptiness filled the room. Nobody said anything, and the atmosphere was so tense I could almost touch it.

"What are you doing here?"

"Whoa, that's such a nice way to greet an old friend. Why don't you sit down—we need to talk."

To my surprise he listened to me and slowly sank down on the other sofa, his eyes on Mia. His jaws were set and his eyes narrow as he said, "What did you tell my wife?"

"Nothing," I said. "But maybe I will." I hadn't intended to threaten him, but I just felt such an overwhelming hatred bubble up inside of me, I couldn't stop the words. "Look, I'm gonna cut straight to the chase," I said. "I know what you did."

His eyes widened, and his lower lip started to shake a little. I looked at him in fascination. It was almost like kicking someone who was already lying down, and I had no plan to stop.

"Mia told me, and I did some research. The statute of limitations has been reached, so you don't need to worry. No jail . . . unfortunately."

He looked confused and scared at the same time. His upper lip was curled like he was about to growl, much like an animal that had gotten pushed into a corner.

"Then . . . why are you here?" He really didn't get it, and I stared at him in disgust.

I didn't feel it was my call to answer and looked at Mia, who finally turned around. Her eyes snapped like lightning, and she held her back straight. I had never seen her this angry before.

"I'm here to hear you apologize."

He licked his lips slowly and grinned. For a second he looked just like I remembered him, only this time with a dirty beard and slightly bigger belly. He looked amused, and I felt like slapping him, but I knew I had to let Mia deal with him herself.

Her voice was calm and steady as she continued: "I'll tell you what you will do. You will go down on your knees and beg me for forgiveness. You will admit what a perverted pig you are and swear I was the only one you harassed. It can never happen again."

"Listen, that was a long time ago . . ."

"Really? For me it feels like yesterday. It even haunts me in my dreams. Do you understand that you destroyed me? I had to leave and see a shrink to be able to move on!" Her voice was loud now, and he nervously looked toward the staircase. He obviously had not told his wife, and if I were he, I would probably not have done so either.

"You disgust me." She got up close to him, and he stood up to get on her level. Then she did something I never expected—the nice girl I knew leaned her head back and placed a big gob of spit by his right eye. His eyes widened, and he breathed heavily through enlarged nostrils. I thought he would hit her, but to our surprise he didn't do anything, just went for a paper towel before he sat down again. I guess he knew he deserved it.

"Look, I was young. I'm not proud of that moment." When she didn't say anything he started to plead.

"OK, OK. I will apologize. Just don't tell my wife and kids." It was a new experience to see him this humble and almost desperate. If only we had confronted him earlier.

"You know what, I won't. I will act as a better person than you have ever been. My only question is why. Why me?"

Peter's shoulders were down, and his whole being looked smaller. He didn't want to look her in the eyes, but she didn't turn away. Eventually he looked at her, and to my surprise he started crying.

"I don't know . . ."

"Really? Do you think I came all this way to hear a shitty explanation like that?"

I was impressed by her confidence. She stood with her back straight, and her voice was firm.

"OK, I wanted to teach you a lesson."

Both Mia and I stared at him like two question marks, and my fists tightened. I wondered what he would do if I punched him.

When we didn't say anything, he continued with a lowered voice. It was like he was ashamed to have the words in his mouth, and what came out was no more than a whisper.

"You rejected me."

Mia leaned forward to hear him better, but I knew she heard him the first time.

"Excuse me?" She spit out her words like they disgusted her.

"You had no respect, you were always calling me out in front of my friends. And that time I asked you out . . . I wasn't kidding." He looked up at her, and his eyes were hopeful, as if he actually thought that his explanation would make her forget his terrible deed. Mia just stared at him for a long time and shook her head like she couldn't believe what she had just heard. When she spoke again, her voice was sharp and cold.

"Down on your knees!"

He looked at her, then me, then back at her. "Are you serious?"

"Do I look like I'm kidding?"

He pursed his lips, and then he actually fell down on his dirty old worker jeans.

"Mia, I'm so sorry. I know I can never make this go away, God knows I have wished for it many times."

He sobbed like a baby, and I almost didn't hear the staircase creak. When I looked up, I saw Karin standing at the top of the stairs. I didn't have to wonder how much of the conversation she had heard; her empty eyes and pale face said it all. Even though she wasn't supposed to know, parts of me were happy the secret was out—she deserved to know the truth. I looked at the man in front of me and realized how pathetic he was. *Try explaining this, you bastard.*

Our job was almost done. Mia started walking toward the door, and a last glance at Peter showed that he was still sobbing but now more quietly. We went out of the house as quickly as possible. It didn't look as idyllic as when we arrived, and we ran the last steps to the car. Even though I wasn't supposed to drive before my treatments had ended, I offered to do so. Mia didn't protest when I took the keys out of her hands. I could tell she was shaken up and decided to find us a hotel somewhere, where she could get some rest. I took out my phone and chose the first one that popped up, and let the GPS guide me.

Mia fell asleep immediately, and after getting off twice at the wrong exit, I finally found the small hotel. Before waking her, I parked the car and then snuck out with my cell phone in a tight grip.

"Hello, yes, I would like to report an assault. I suspect it's a case of wife battering."

The picture of Karin's bruise was stuck in my memory. He had gotten away once—I wouldn't let him get away twice.

CHAPTER 27

The next morning, we didn't leave the hotel room. At one point we ordered room service, but when the food arrived neither of us had any appetite. It was a big room, but we sat side by side in the double bed, with our backs to the headboard. We didn't move for hours, both trying to grasp what had happened. I was still mad at myself. How could I not have known? Even though Mia hadn't told me, I should have had a more sensitive ear, I should have known something was wrong. I felt like a huge failure as a friend, even though I realized there was no point in grieving then. I just wished she had told me right away. I wasn't sure what fourteen-year-old Anna would have done, but I hoped she would have had the strength to convince Mia to go to the police. Peter could have been behind bars right then, and I was furious.

Everything started to make sense, though. All the times I had missed her, devastated that she hadn't written, wondering why she'd waited until the very last minute before telling me her family was leaving. I thought I had done something to make her upset, but I realized now how selfish I had been. I should have understood that it was bigger than me, that something wasn't right. She wasn't running from me—she was running from her old life.

"I'm sorry I wasn't there." My voice was a bit hoarse after not having talked for a long time.

Mia turned to me and shook her head so hard that her ponytail jumped up and down. "It wasn't your fault!"

"I know—I just wish there was something I could have done."

She just shook her head again, slowly this time. She chewed on her lip and seemed distant, as if she'd thought of something. When she finally spoke again, her face was tense.

"All this time I have wondered why."

"Does it feel better now that you know?" I was afraid I had made it all worse by dragging her there.

She didn't reply at first. She seemed deep in thought, and her eyes were empty, not focused on anything in front of her. A small teardrop ran down her cheek. I waited patiently and resisted an impulse to hug her.

"It does. My psychologist told me that to be able to move on I needed to accept what happened and look forward. And I tried, I really did." She looked at me with tear-filled eyes and opened her arms for me to give her a long hug.

"I know, sweetie, I know," I whispered in her hair, rocking her from side to side. When her nose got blocked, I went to get a tissue.

She blew her nose before she continued. "I believe she was right—you shouldn't dwell on the past. But on the other hand, I have always wondered why, and if I could have done anything to prevent it."

"And now that you know?" I was afraid where this was going.

"Now that I know . . ." She blew her nose one more time. "I wouldn't have done anything differently."

She sat up a bit straighter, and her eyes glowed rebelliously. Her face had turned red from weeping, but she didn't seem to care. She looked like the obstinate and proud girl I knew.

"If I can't speak my mind and stand up against people who do wrong, then what kind of person would I be?"

"You're right. I guess Peter's ego couldn't handle it."

"You know, in the beginning I almost let him destroy me. I cried every night, and I felt disgusted with myself."

Hearing how hard it had been for her made me so angry that I bit my tongue until I could feel the taste of blood in my mouth.

"It felt good to stand in front of him and show him that he didn't break me."

I studied her lean appearance. Her thin arms reminded me of tiny chicken wings. She looked as fragile as she did when we were kids, but she sat with her head high, and I admired her strength.

She looked restlessly around the room before she got up and put the hotel kettle on. "Tea?"

I nodded and stretched my arms. My feet had almost fallen asleep, and I shook them to give them some life back. I went to the bathroom, and when I got back Mia was sitting in the bed again, with two teacups. She handed me one, and I sat down and blew some air into it. I disappeared in thought. How proud I was to have a friend like Mia! I didn't know anyone else with the same courage.

"How do you feel about tomorrow?" Mia's voice brought me back to the hotel room. I had tried to not think about it, but the question reminded me of what was to come. At first I didn't feel the pain in my stomach, but it came crawling, like when you accidentally put your hand on a hot stove: for the first few seconds the pain is so intense you can't feel it, and then it burns like nothing you've ever felt before.

The sudden pain surprised me a bit. I had not had any stomach issues since I'd been on sick leave.

"Well, I would avoid it if I could," I croaked, and looked at her with puppy eyes. A tiny part of me wished she would allow me to sit this one out. She held her teacup with one hand and put her free arm around me. I leaned my head against her shoulder, trying to soak up some of her strength.

She must have felt how stiff I was and said softly, "You know what, we have two stops close to one another. If you want, we can do the least painful one first."

I nodded and felt relieved, even though I knew it would last only a day. It was my turn to face my demons, and compared with what Mia just had been through, it would be nothing.

CHAPTER 28

When I woke up the next day, the room was empty. Mia had left a small note on the nightstand, saying that she was downstairs in the breakfast room. The word "breakfast" made my stomach rumble. I always considered breakfast the best meal of the day. It made you feel good after sleeping for several hours, it was easy to prepare, and you ate it with the whole day still in front of you. What wasn't to like?

I rolled out of bed and jumped in the shower. I carefully removed my hairpiece, which made me look like I had longer hair than I'd ever had before. It was a bit ironic; I had always wanted thick, long hair, and life had given it to me under the weirdest circumstances. As long as I didn't look like a pale cancer patient, I was happy enough, and I wished it would continue that way. My oncologist had warned me that the anti-nausea tablets would make me gain weight, but it hadn't shown yet, and I'd decided not to worry about it. After all, I preferred a few extra pounds to whole days filled with nausea that left me empty and weak. I washed the little hair I had left with baby shampoo, and I did the best I could to avoid touching the scar.

I found Mia with her nose in her phone, zooming in and out on the map of Sweden. She looked up.

"It's fascinating how spread out this country is. We have been driving like crazy, and we are not even a third from the south end."

"That should mean we are not far from our next stop." I grabbed a piece of toast but then dropped it. I had decided to only eat fat and protein, no carbs. Maybe it seemed weird, but there was research showing that cancer cells died in fat but thrived on sugar. The ketogenic diet was debated, and you could say what you wanted to, but I wasn't in a position to take any chances. My decision meant a big no to several dishes I loved, and I was still adjusting. I sighed and went over to the breakfast buffet, where I loaded scrambled eggs onto my plate while giving the scones and jam a wishful look.

"It should not be more than about two hours to Stockholm." Mia put down her phone and went for another cup of coffee.

I noticed there were no other people around us and looked at the clock on the wall. Half past ten. If I was not mistaken, checkout was at ten, and breakfast should have stopped being served a while back. Mia noticed my look and winked at me. "I made us a deal."

Before the operation, things like this had made me uncomfortable. I didn't like to be late, and rules were rules—at least I thought so. But if you think about it, what difference did it make? Is it worth raising your heartbeat, causing a stomachache by shoveling your breakfast into your mouth, or, even worse, skipping it altogether, just to try to catch up on some lost minutes? I decided it wasn't, even though I probably would tip the kitchen personnel a bit extra before we left.

***

Looking out the car window, I thought of the last time I had seen Mrs. Wallenius. We had grabbed a drink at a rooftop bar near Vasagatan and had admired a beautiful view of the center of Stockholm. I was still studying at the time, and I'm pretty sure the meetings of the mentorship program I was enrolled in were not supposed to take place in bars, but Mrs. Wallenius had always done what she wanted to. She was strong willed by nature and didn't care about anyone's opinion. Maybe that's why she enjoyed such a successful career. She had started out as a banker at one of the biggest firms in Stockholm and now owned her own company, which had received the Gasell Award two years in a row, meaning she had one of the fastest-growing companies in the region. As if that weren't enough, she ranked high on the list of the one hundred most powerful women in Sweden. I know some of my fellow students would have killed to meet her. She usually didn't have time to help students, but she met me as a favor to one of my favorite professors, who must have put in a good word for me. I didn't know her well; we met up only a few times, but that was enough for her to give me good advice for how to get a head start as a young woman in the business world. We got along well, and I would almost dare to say that she liked me, even though she was good at hiding her feelings. When I moved to Dublin for the job, our meet-ups had stopped naturally, but I had kept a close eye on her company and its development ever since. She'd been my ultimate role model, and I remembered how I'd wished to be just like her. I was never sure I would be able to; she was known to be efficient and ruthless, a cold businesswoman who didn't take no for an answer. There was nothing that she wanted that she didn't get eventually.

I had never questioned how she lived her life, the sacrifices she must have made to get where she was, but my new situation had made me curious. How did she do it all? I knew she had a young son, whom she rarely talked about, and a husband who worked for the government. I realized she might be traveling for work and decided to look up her number on my phone. It was probably best to make an appointment. Her receptionist answered and said that Mrs. Wallenius had a packed schedule all week, but that he would make sure she got my message. That meant we would spend a few days not focusing on our mission in the capital, which wasn't all that bad—after all, we had another person to meet, too.

The car ride went faster than I'd thought it would, and we stopped for lunch before heading to the hotel. I went to sleep like the granny I had become, and Mia went out shopping.

I was awoken by the phone ringing. To my surprise it was Mrs. Wallenius, calling me in person. She kept it short like always and set a time that very same night, the same cocktail bar as before.

I did my best to look professional; it was a pretty fancy place, and I knew Mrs. Wallenius didn't like sloppy people in general. When I showed up, she was already seated, taking small sips of whiskey and looking through her calendar. The bartender showed me the bottle of Irish Teeling, and it took all of my willpower to turn it down. I wasn't supposed to drink with so many chemicals in my body, which is why I ordered tea and felt like the most boring person in the world. Mrs. Wallenius didn't comment on it, and I sat down quickly. I knew she didn't have all night.

Her lips were carefully painted in a wine-red color, which matched her nails perfectly. Her gray suit looked expensive, as did her jewelry. She had a natural sense of commanding presence. I had wondered many times how she did it, and so far I had concluded it must be her way of looking totally uninterested and calm in all situations. That, in combination with her proud posture, made her a powerful woman. I felt privileged to have her sitting opposite me.

"Anna! Good to see you again. How are you keeping?" I knew she didn't want to know about my personal life; the question was for me to give her an update on my current job situation and next steps. Normally I would have prepared several hours before the meeting, listing both questions and an update of my five-year career plan in a document that I would have sent her twenty minutes before we met. This time I had purposely not sent her anything. I knew that would make her annoyed, but this time was different. I hoped she would understand.

"I'm rethinking this whole career thing." I said it quickly and then held my breath, afraid of her reaction.

For a second she looked like I had punched her in the stomach. She went back to her neutral facial expression pretty quickly, though, and took a sip of her whiskey before answering. "And what are you planning to do instead, if I may ask?"

"I don't know . . ." I knew this was one of the sentences she hated the most, but I had no energy to come up with a suitable lie. "I have always looked for the next step on the career ladder, you know that. It has all been about proving myself, and until now I thought that gave me a sense of satisfaction."

"But?"

"It doesn't anymore. I've discovered so many other aspects of life that I value more, and I don't think I can put in the same effort as before."

She looked at me like I had just said something disgraceful.

"Can I ask you something?" I didn't wait for her reply. "I know you've worked hard to get to where you are, and now, when you seem to have it all, are you satisfied?"

Maybe I imagined it, but she seemed puzzled by the direction this conversation was going. Her answers didn't come as fast as they normally did, and she started to fiddle with her wedding ring.

"I believe there are always more interesting levels to reach. You're never done."

"All those long nights of work, the worry that comes with having your own company, the time away from family . . ." I took a deep breath and almost didn't dare look at her before I dropped the question that had been burning in the back of my throat the whole time. "Is it worth it?"

She was silent for a while, to the point where I wondered if she would reply at all.

"You need to rephrase that question."

I was puzzled. She would have been a successful politician, turning questions around like that.

"The question should not be if it is worth it or not in general. You need to dig deeper. What's worth it for me might not be worth it for you. It's all about what you value in life."

Of course she was right. I felt more stupid than usual in her company.

"To your question . . . I'm going to tell you something I've never told anyone before."

Boy, was she good at keeping momentum up. I leaned forward and waited like a hungry bird.

"In the beginning of my career . . . no, it wasn't worth it. Not because the work is not the number one priority in my life—you know it is—but because I didn't believe in what I was doing. I didn't know what I wanted, and I didn't feel any meaningfulness. I did my work because it looked good in the eyes of others, and I wanted to be admired." She stirred her glass so all the scents would rise to the surface, then emptied it in one go.

"You will never be happy if you do things for others, Anna. When I started working for myself, which I did long before I had my own company, it became worth it."

"Working for yourself?" I felt ashamed to ask, but I knew I might not get another chance to talk to her, so what the hell.

"You need to find the reason you are working. Even if it is to be able to pay the bills, you need to find something more, another reason. Then it becomes less about work and more about self-development. The way I see it, I get paid for learning new things every day."

I'd never thought of it like that before—in my world, the word "work" was synonymous with pressure and the fear of not being good enough. I must say, Mrs. Wallenius's mind-set was more appealing. I made a mental note to try her way of thinking when I got back from my long-term sick leave. After all, every situation gets better if you view it as an opportunity and not as a must.

She looked at her watch, and I knew my time was up. She closed her hands on the table in front of her and fixed me with her eyes, making sure she had my full attention. "It's all about being able to lay on your deathbed not wishing you had done anything differently."

I wanted to tell her that such a day might be closer than I wanted, but I decided not to share my thoughts with her. After all, this was a business meeting.

"Anna. I know I always look ahead and plan for the future, but a big part of being successful is to have respect for yourself. If you don't take the personal time you need, you won't last long, and that's a safe road to a short career."

On the way out, the bartender called a cab, and it was ready by the time the elevator door opened on the first floor. I saw her disappear around the corner and considered what she had said. It wasn't rocket science; it all made sense. There and then, in the lobby of a hotel in the capital of Sweden, I decided that I didn't want to look back at my life, old or not so old, and see someone who chose her work over herself. I started walking back to the hotel, enjoying the silence.

CHAPTER 29

The next day I was so nervous I couldn't eat anything. I kept fiddling with my napkin till Mia put her hand on top of mine to make me stop.

"It'll be all right. You'll see."

"You know I keep asking myself if this is necessary."

"Anna." She said my name slowly, as to warn me. "This whole journey is about going outside your comfort zone, and nobody said it would be easy."

"I know, I know."

I stopped ripping the napkins apart but immediately started turning the salt and pepper shakers over instead. She rolled her eyes, and I could tell it was driving her crazy, but I couldn't help myself. My heart was flickering like I'd had too many espressos, even though the only thing standing in front of me was a glass of water. Mia went up and got a plate filled with eggs, then put it in front of me.

"Eat."

I sighed deeply and picked up the fork. I had started this, and I had to finish it. Hopefully he wasn't even in town. People go on vacation all the time.

As if she had read my mind, she put down her teacup. "I called his office. He is in town."

Shit. There was no turning back now. I put down my fork. "I'll go and start making myself ready."

She nailed me with her gaze, cleared her throat, and pointed toward my plate.

"Oh, right." I shoveled down the eggs while standing up, and then hurried off. Mia stayed, and I knew I should have waited for her to finish her tea, but I couldn't sit still any longer.

***

Back in the hotel room, I studied myself in the bathroom mirror. Except for the wig, you couldn't really tell that something was wrong. That made me a bit calmer. I didn't plan on telling him about my situation. I had to tell him something important, and I didn't want sympathy to cloud his judgment. While spending more time than usual on my makeup, I thought of why I was so hopelessly in love with him, even after all these years. It wasn't just one thing, of course. He had always been brave and not afraid of speaking up, a trait I admired. We used to bash heads in classroom discussions every now and then, debating different political standpoints. I wasn't sure whether I pissed him off or not, but I loved it. That was the only time I got his attention. He had a lot of friends and spent most of his time playing soccer. I never saw him with a girl, though, and I believe he was as shy as I was when it came to dating. He was a kind soul, and I could think of numerous times that I watched him help his friends out. I especially remember the time he stood up against Peter to save a friend from school. If I had to point out a day when he got my attention for real, that was it. He got pretty badly beaten and had limped for a week, but I'd never heard him complain.

I leaned closer to the mirror to get the eye shadow right. I tried to picture him in front of me. Last time I saw him, he had the same boyish face as always, but his stubble and Adam's apple suggested a young man. With his big blue eyes and dark curly hair, he looked a lot like his Spanish dad, even though Carl was taller. When we were kids he had been thin, almost skinny. That changed once we grew older and he started hitting the gym. The last time I'd seen him had been one year earlier during a business trip, in a bar in the city center. I almost didn't recognize him in his suit, he looked so grown-up. When he turned around, I had immediately recognized his dimples, though. I had always thought he was cute, but he had never been the one to turn heads in school. Now, however, he could have easily fit into a Calvin Klein advertisement or the like. His most attractive aspect, though, was the fact that he was not aware of his looks. *Some guys are full of themselves, but he's nothing like that*, I thought dreamily while looking for the mascara in my little makeup bag.

"You done?" Mia slammed the door and popped her head into the bathroom. "I need to pee."

When she saw my efforts, she added, "Wow, you look nice!" She studied my face and exclaimed, "Maybe I need to put in some effort, too, otherwise I won't be able to walk next to you!"

"Come on, it's only some mascara." I got embarrassed and left the room. I laid on my stomach on the bed with my legs crossed, pretending to browse through my phone. God, I really acted like a teenager!

"If you say so . . ." She locked the door, and I immediately jumped up and started to look through my clothes for the fifth time. Maybe I should go with the dress instead of jeans? Or was that too fancy for an average day? I decided that it probably was and put it down again. When Mia came out, we both looked around to be sure not to leave anything behind, then we went to check out.

***

We stood in front of the tall office building feeling small. The street outside was empty except for an occasional man or woman in a suit passing by. The entrance was big, and I hoped it would open automatically. I wasn't sure that my shaky hands could handle a heavy door. Mia stood next to me, making sure I didn't escape. She pushed me toward the door, which thankfully opened right away. She gave me a quick hug.

"I'll leave you to it. See you for lunch, OK?"

I nodded and went inside. I found myself in a peaceful room lit by the sunlight shining through the high glass ceiling. In the middle was a big fountain surrounded by green plants and some small pink flowers. The rippling sound was calming, and if I hadn't seen people in suits in the escalator behind it, I wouldn't have believed it was an office; it looked more like a museum. On the left there was a beautiful desk made out of marble with a girl behind it looking as neat as the room. With her dark-gray, tailor-made suit, she fit right in. She was so focused on the computer in front of her that my first thought was that she must be a part of the furnishings. She must have felt me staring and looked up.

"May I help you?" With her shiny blond hair neatly tucked away behind her ears, she reminded me of a Barbie doll. I almost wanted to touch her to make sure she wasn't made out of plastic.

"Yes, I'm looking for Carl Svensson."

"And you are?"

"Anna Larsson."

"Do you have an appointment?"

"No . . . but I'm an old friend."

She studied me a few seconds too long, and I felt how she was judging my choice of clothing. With my leather jacket and jeans, I didn't really fit in.

"Well, if he's not expecting you . . . I'm afraid you'll have to wait until I get a hold of him. Please take a seat." She nodded toward a suite of furniture at the other end of the room, as far away from her as possible. *A weird way of welcoming visitors*, I thought and then sat down on the gray sofa. It was like sitting on a hard bench, and I guessed it was more for show than comfort. I waited a good half hour and had to remind myself not to be upset—after all, I'd shown up unannounced. I tried to sit with my legs crossed and back straight, in an attempt to look like one of those casual and feminine women from an ad. I gave up after a few minutes and placed both feet on the floor, leaning my arms on my thighs. I looked down on my white Converse, studying the latest stains.

It's funny how you sometimes can sense when someone is watching you. It didn't fail this time, either. When I looked up, my stomach jumped; it reminded me of the feeling you get when you go on a ride in an amusement park. The adrenaline started to pump through my veins, and I had to force myself to take a deep breath before I stood up.

"Anna?"

"Hi." My voice was brittle, and I regretted I hadn't prepared something better to say.

He hesitated before giving me an awkward hug. It lasted for only a few seconds, and I wished he had held on a bit longer.

"Are you here for business?" He looked puzzled and seemed to think really hard. "Did we have a meeting scheduled?" There was a tremble in his voice, as if we really had a meeting and he'd forgotten.

"No, no. I was just in the neighborhood." I heard how weak the lie was and realized I needed a better explanation or I would have to put all my cards on the table. My imagination was limited, and I decided the latter was a better strategy. "Look, it's a long story. Do you have a few minutes?"

He looked at his wristwatch. "Yeah, why not? Let's go across the road, though, they have better coffee."

As we walked out, I could feel his eyes on me, and I would have given my left hand to have heard his thoughts.

***

"Why don't you take a seat while I order? Espresso, tea . . . what do you prefer?" He peered at the big menu above the counter.

"A cappuccino would be great, thanks."

He turned to the barista while I tried to find a quiet area in the back. The place was not crowded, but I still didn't want the few people who were there to hear us. I found two armchairs in a corner. Perfect.

He looked like I had imagined, even though his loose shirt indicated that he didn't visit the gym as often as before. He still looked good, and I smiled when he tried to balance a tray with two cups of coffee while not knocking down someone's jacket on the way.

He sighed in relief when he put the cups down without spilling anything, then looked up and gave me a broad smile that showed his perfect teeth. "I can't believe you're here! It's really good to see you."

Good because it was a year ago, or good because you are secretly in love with me, too? My thoughts went nuts, and I tried to stay calm. Cool people don't talk too much, I reminded myself and tried to look indifferent. It only resulted in him putting his head to the side in confusion, and I assumed my attempt made me look angry instead. I closed my eyes and took a deep breath for what felt like the hundredth time that day. I had to stop acting like a fifteen-year-old girl!

We made small talk for a bit, and I told him I was just visiting some friends, taking some days off work.

"Good for you. We all need a break sometimes."

You have no idea, I thought as I tried to smile. "Look, I know it's weird, me showing up like this."

He made a weak attempt to say that it wasn't, but I could tell it was a polite lie.

"It's just that I've had a lot of time to think, and there is something I need to tell you."

"Sounds intriguing." He leaned forward, and I damned his good looks for distracting me.

"I've decided to be more frank with people."

"OK." His dimples showed again.

Great, here I am, pouring my heart out, and he's clearly amused. Then again, maybe I would have been, too, if I had been in his shoes. I didn't know how long we had before he had to head back to the office, and I decided to spit it out. Now or never. "Just do it," like the Nike slogan says.

"I like you."

It was as though he couldn't decide how to react, and his smile showed one dimple instead of two. "I like you, too."

"No, no, not like that. I mean . . . I really like you."

He sat up straighter and ran his hand through his hair. His eyes started to wander, and when he finally looked at me again, I could swear they had dropped a bit.

"What do you mean?"

"I've always had a crush on you, and . . . I still have." I didn't dare look at him and got a steadier grip around the cup in front of me. All of a sudden he put his hands on mine. They were warm, and I wished he would never pull them away.

"Anna . . . I'm getting married in the fall."

His words burned like an opened wound. I pulled my hands away and met his eyes, which were now more intense. I blinked and looked away. My lips were clenched, and I looked at his hands. How could I not have noticed the ring on his finger?

"That's . . . great." I tried my best to look happy, but I felt that the tears were not far away.

He looked stressed, like he couldn't make up his mind how to handle the situation. Poor guy. I'd really caught him unprepared.

"Yeah, it is. We're very happy."

I swallowed hard and tried another smile. My jaw hurt, and it didn't feel natural at all.

"Then I'm happy for you. Congrats!"

"Anna, I'm sorry." He looked me straight in the eyes and nailed me with his gaze. I could not look away, or escape.

"I'm sorry, too. It was stupid to surprise you like this, but I guess I just wanted you to know. I realized that we go through life with so many things unsaid, and I wanted to be a bit braver for once."

"I respect that." He was now serious, and I can't describe how thankful I was that he didn't make fun of me. We didn't say anything for a while, me because I was mortified and he because he was caught up in thoughts. Finally he seemed ready to say something.

"Do you know I was interested in you in high school?"

What? I felt my face get red even though I tried to hide how mad I was. What right did he have to mess with me like this? It must have been clear I didn't believe him, and he tried to explain.

"I was too insecure to tell you."

I studied his facial expression and had to admit there was no sign of a smile—he was actually quite serious. His gaze became unfocused, and his posture relaxed, as if he were thinking back on something. I loosened up a bit; maybe he was telling the truth after all.

He leaned back in his chair and put out his arms in a gesture of resignation. "How funny is life? I mean, imagine what could have happened if we were a bit more honest with each other."

I didn't say anything, and I didn't want him to speculate, either. It hurt, and I felt a sudden need to get up. The air was too thick, and I wanted out.

"Carl, I need to go." I stood up a bit too fast, and the table swayed and the half-full cups almost fell to the floor. He steadied it at the last minute and looked at me with curious eyes.

"You leaving already?"

"Mm. I apologize for this, and I hope the wedding will be nice." I mumbled good-bye and hurried away without hugging him. I needed to get out. Now.

***

Since we had checked out, I had nowhere to go, and it wasn't time to meet Mia just yet. I wandered the streets randomly, trying to sort my thoughts out. The situation felt like it had been taken straight out of a movie, and I was in the less desirable position. I tried to decide what I felt. Sadness and jealousy, of course, but there was something else, too. Looking out over the waters of Kungsholmen, one of my favorite areas in Stockholm, I tried to figure out what it was. An older couple was walking by, holding hands. It moved me to see how they still seemed to be fond of each other, after what I guessed had been a lifetime together. I wondered how they'd met, and then I felt a need to walk faster. I knew now what I felt; the frustration went through my whole body and made my fingertips itch.

I was fully aware that it might not have worked out between Carl and me, and that would have been fine. That's life, and it wasn't the reason for my feelings. The annoying fact was that I would never know. I wondered how many people's paths were never crossed because of fear and insecurity. Most couples I knew had met because of a coincidence, and imagine what would have happened if they hadn't grasped the opportunity then and there. If they hadn't, there would be less love in the world.

My frustration turned to anger—I was mad at myself for not being braver. What had I been afraid of? To be turned down, humiliated, exposed . . . It was ironic how fast I came up with a list of reasons. I wasn't sure if we could ever cut out all fear from our lives, but I did know that we could choose how big a part we let it have in our decisions. I remembered a TED Talk about how to become successful that I had seen on YouTube a while back. One of the success factors the speaker mentioned was not being afraid of failing. It had sounded like a cliché at the time, but now it made perfect sense.

I looked at my wristwatch and realized it was almost time to meet Mia. I took one last glance at the beautiful view in front of me. The sea was so still, the sun was shining on the trees on the other side, and in the distance a small bridge stretched over the water, glittering like jewelry. As I crossed the road by the train station I felt lighter, heading for Plattan and the Concert Hall Restaurant, where Mia and I were to meet for lunch.

CHAPTER 30

The next day we left the capital and headed southwest. Our goal was Varberg, a small city by the sea where I had spent most of my childhood summers. It was beautiful and a safe place to let kids run free. Like most cities in Sweden, it wasn't big; I guessed it had around thirty thousand inhabitants. Probably more during the summer, though—that's when the place really livened up, with its cozy restaurants, family-friendly atmosphere, and nice beaches.

My family on my mother's side lived there, but I knew I wouldn't have the energy to meet all of them at once. There was one person in particular I wanted to see. I always felt guilty for not visiting her more often, especially after I moved abroad and had limited vacation days. That was a poor excuse, and I knew it. The truth was that I could have gone home for just a weekend, but I chose flashy weekend trips in Europe instead. I told myself that I needed to live my life and that I would visit later. *Later.* That word had a whole new meaning nowadays. If there were a way of starting all over again and doing things differently, I would have used it to set my priorities straight. Once they had been, all my decisions would have been easier to make. I valued my family highly, but I had a feeling I didn't show it. The fact that I used to choose a party weekend over someone who had been there for my whole life and now needed me was outrageous. I'm not saying I should have limited myself and my passion for traveling completely, but to visit someone dear once a year is just not enough. It felt good that I had come to my senses, and I leaned back and stared out the window. It would be a long ride.

Neither of us had the patience to sit for five hours straight in the car, so we made a stop for lunch. We found a classic *värdshus*, a restaurant and inn along a motorway. This one didn't look like much at first glance, but it was quite cozy inside. Everything from the walls to the ceiling lamps seemed to be made out of a light, golden type of wood. The only exceptions were the small red curtains with white embroidery. As much as I found it cozy, I couldn't help thinking of the fire risk. I seemed to be the only one having such thoughts, though; the place was packed with people. It served big steaks and fish fillets with creamy sauces and potatoes, the kind of heavy food you expect travelers to need after a long day on the road. We found a corner booth and had a look at the menu. I sighed. There was so much good stuff I couldn't eat because of the new diet. Well, if it could keep me alive I guessed it would be worth it. I told myself it was for the best and asked the waitress to exchange the fries for extra spinach.

"Do you think she will remember you?"

My thoughts were still with the food, and I looked at Mia with puzzled eyes. I tried to make the paper menu stand on the table by itself, but knocked it over twice before I looked over at her.

"Of course she will!"

"Well, you told me she has shown signs of Alzheimer's."

"Yeah, she has a hard time remembering new things; her short-term memory is pretty bad. Usually she remembers things from back in the day."

"OK... I don't wanna sound mean, but if she won't remember we were there... is there any point in visiting?"

My eyes got even smaller, and I resisted an impulse to tell her how rude it was to suggest such a thing. I knew I couldn't be mad at her, because the thought had crossed my mind, too.

"I know. The thing is, though, that she is such a nice and positive person, and there is no reason not to make a few of her days special."

"Speaking of living in the now..."

I leaned back and gave her a thumbs-up. "I'm sure she can teach us a thing or two about that."

The waitress interrupted and served us two plates with enormous chicken fillets. Half of Mia's plate was covered with fries, and I saw by the look on her face that she would never be able to eat it all. Well, if I knew her right, she would at least give it a good try.

***

A few hours later we pulled up the driveway to the home for the elderly. I never liked these places; they felt like the people in them had given up on life and were just waiting around for their last breaths. I had to admit that the staff at this home had done a good job to make the wait for the inevitable more pleasant, with the small fountain by the entrance and the carefully planted roses.

There was no problem finding an empty parking space, and we were soon on our way into one of the buildings. I couldn't tell if it was my memory or imagination, but I recognized one of the nurses. She was robust with crude orange hair, and she seemed more interested in polishing her nails than in talking to us. Apparently we had interrupted the afternoon tea, and she advised us to wait in Grandma's room in the meantime. Her unwelcoming attitude annoyed me, but I let it slip. I knew the residents' daily routines were important, and thus we obliged and headed toward the end of the hallway.

"Oh, this is so cozy!" Mia exclaimed when she entered the little room. I had been there before and had never thought of it. Now I looked around and tried to see it through her eyes. She was right; it was like coming home to somebody's living room, and it didn't look at all like the sterile common areas. The walls were covered with heavy oil paintings in robust wooden frames. The dark mahogany mirror to our right stood out for its craftsmanship; you could tell somebody had put his heart and soul into making it. The light beige sofa in front of us looked inviting, and so we sat down on the embroidered golden flowers. The latest gossip magazines were laid out on the coffee table, and I wondered if my grandmother was able to read them. Her sight had gotten much worse over the last couple of years. My eyes kept wandering around. It was more of a small apartment than a room, apart from the fact that the bed was in the living room. I guess Grandma didn't need much space anyway, and I was pleased that they had made it look just like her old place. We were browsing through the latest news on the royal family when the door opened and my eighty-five-year-old grandma slowly walked toward us with her walker on wheels as support.

"Such a nice surprise!" Her wrinkled, slightly round face lit up with the sight of us. She was so cute, with her silver-gray hair neatly combed into a bob. She wore pearls around her neck that went great with her navy blue cardigan. I was always impressed she still had the energy to care about her appearance, but I guess some things never change, especially not when you worked in the fashion industry your whole life.

Her hearing wasn't the best, and I introduced Mia in a rather loud voice. I had forgotten how short she was, and I had to bend down to be able to give her a hug. Her tiny shoulders felt smaller than I remembered, and I got worried that she didn't eat enough.

"Did you arrive today?" Her smile revealed slightly stained teeth, probably a result of years of coffee drinking. I squeezed her hands. They were wrinkled and crooked, telling a story in themselves of a hardworking woman.

"Yes, we wanted to see you. How are you keeping?"

"Oh, they are taking great care of me, such dolls. Even when I forget their names they are nice!"

One of the reasons she had reached this impressive age must have been her positive attitude. She seldom complained, and I knew the nurses adored her.

Her green eyes peered at us, and she seemed genuinely interested as she leaned forward. "Did you arrive today?"

This was what I had been afraid of. Her memory had gotten worse these past few years, and it was hard to keep a normal conversation going.

"Yes, Grandma, we're just visiting for the day."

She smacked her lips in delight. "If I knew you were coming, I would have prepared coffee. I haven't had any today!"

We resisted the urge to tell her she'd just come from afternoon tea, and Mia went up to the small kitchen behind the bed to prepare some more. I didn't correct her—one more cup wouldn't hurt.

"I have cookies, too! In the cupboard." Grandma had always had a sweet tooth, and now she pointed with a shaky finger in the direction of the sink. Then she turned to me, her eyes sparkling. "You know, it doesn't matter at my age—I don't have to look skinny anymore." She giggled like a mischievous little girl. Oh, how I had missed her! She was my role model when it came to taking one day at a time and enjoying the small things to the fullest.

If she loved anything, it was to socialize and play card games with friends, and it was a shame that even that had gotten too tiring for her. I got an idea and jumped up to see if the electric wheelchair was available. It would be too demanding to go for a walk, but with the wheelchair we would be able to take her outside. The grumpy nurse showed me how it worked, and we decided to go for a walk in a nearby park.

The small pond I had in mind was not far away, but with our pace it took us a good twenty minutes to reach it. The nurse had given us some bread to feed to the ducks, but the seagulls hovering over us seemed interested, too. The sun was shining, and there was no breeze: a perfect summer day. Grandma and I found a bench while Mia tried not to get attacked by all the birds while rationing out the bread crumbs.

My grandma closed her eyes and turned her face toward the sun. She took a deep breath and inhaled the fresh air, which smelled of newly cut grass. She looked at peace with nature, and when she didn't move for a few minutes, I almost thought she'd fallen asleep. A quick squeeze of her hands told me she hadn't. Her head lifted, and her chuckles made me warm inside. It seemed like she enjoyed watching the small battle between Mia and the persistent seagulls.

After a while I felt the urge to get up; it was like something had crawled under my skin. The sun was nice and all, but I had always been a restless soul. The peaceful look on my grandma's face made me stay put. I had to pull myself together; I wasn't a small kid, after all.

It was like Grandma could tell how I felt, because she turned to me with an amused pair of eyes. "Difficulties sitting still?"

"It's fine." The lie came a bit too fast.

"I could sit here all day."

I had to tighten my jaw not to look like I'd just seen a horror movie. She laughed at my devastated expression.

"There is so much to look at, haven't you noticed?"

I followed her gaze but didn't agree. Yes, it was sunny and the pond was filled with birds, but there was nothing I had not seen before. To me it all looked pretty normal and, to be honest, boring.

"Let me tell you what I see." She paused for effect and let her eyes go over the small pond once more.

"Life and friendship." She sat up a bit straighter and gave me a big smile that told me she was happy with her observation. I met her energetic, small eyes, which reminded me of a squirrel's. I had no idea what she was talking about. Until then, I had thought it was only her memory that was bad, but maybe she was really losing it. She didn't mind my confusion; in fact, she almost seemed to enjoy it.

"This pond was not always here, you see. It was more of a . . . swamp. A dirty and forgotten place where no one came to visit. When they cleaned it up, it didn't take long before both animals and people gathered. Look how it gives life and joy!"

She pointed at the far end of the other side of the pond where a swan was graciously bending her neck to drink the water. Her mate swam toward her, and together they started circling the pond. As crazy as it sounds, it seemed like the other smaller birds showed their respect: they quickly moved out of the way when the swans approached them. A soft pull of my cardigan moved my attention to the left. My grandma put her fingers to her lips and nodded in the direction of the reeds that surrounded most of the pond. At first I didn't see anything in particular, and once more I questioned my grandma's sanity. As I was about to give up, I saw something moving and almost stopped breathing. From the grass a downy little head popped up, followed by a tiny yellow body with black stains. He was circling around something, and at first I couldn't see what it was. When I looked closer it seemed like the small duckling had a friend.

"They lost their mom and siblings a while ago."

I blinked rapidly. "How? That's sad."

"I believe one of them is stuck, but that's not the point. There were at least five more of them that kept going with their mom. She didn't notice what happened, but this small fellow did. And the beauty is that he decided to stay."

"That's true friendship." All she had told me started to make sense.

"I have to help them." I stood up, but Grandma put her hand on my arm.

"You can, but that will make them smell of human, and the mom might not touch them again."

"I'll take my chances," I said and reached for her gloves in the small basket of the wheelchair. Slowly, not to scare them, I approached the small friends. When I got close, the little one made an attempt to bite my hand, and I admired his courage. Here I was, ten times his size, and he still tried to defend his buddy. He couldn't hurt me with the gloves on, and I started digging a bigger hole around his friend. It seemed like his foot was stuck. It didn't take long to remove the small root that kept him back. The two ducklings disappeared quickly into the water, and I brushed the soil from my hands.

Coming back to my grandma, I couldn't help grinning like I'd gotten fooled on April first. She had been right all the time.

"Life and friendship, huh?"

"Life and friendship," she repeated happily and stretched her legs, apparently very pleased with herself.

I was quiet for a bit. We had had the exact same view; yet we had observed completely different things. How could that be? I couldn't get rid of the question, and so I finally turned to her.

"Grandma, can I ask you something?"

She moved her weight around on the bench before she seemed comfortable enough. "Anytime."

"How do you do it? I mean . . . you seem to appreciate every day and moment, no matter what happens."

Her left eyebrow raised, and I could tell she had expected something else. "Oh, dear, that's not that hard. I simply take the time to do it."

My slack expression and empty eyes made her elaborate.

"Your generation seems to be in such a hurry all the time. And if you're not, you're always on your phones. Of course you won't see the whole picture."

Ironically, Mia came walking toward us, typing on her cell phone. She sat down without taking her eyes off it.

I bit my lip and turned away. I knew she was right, and I wondered how many moments had passed me by because I hadn't been present. I thought of all the days I had rushed to work, between meetings, to and from the gym. Not once had I stopped to look around me or take in my surroundings. I was running through life as if it were a competition. It's true that professional sprinters would get to the goal faster than an average runner, but they would never have the time to enjoy the track.

I heard my grandma speaking to Mia.

"Did we meet, my dear?"

I sighed deeply. It was a pity her memory played these games, but I felt grateful that we had decided to come and visit.

Underneath her confused appearance was a very wise woman. I wished to have the same insights at her age—if I ever reached it, that is.

I made a sign to Mia that it was time to leave. I didn't want to get Grandma tired, and so the three of us headed back at an ambling pace, with Grandma in the wheelchair. The slow walk would normally have made me crazy, but now I tried to take in my surroundings the same way my grandma did. Once you accept that life is no race, there is no need to stress. We will all get to the finish line sooner or later.

***

Back in the car, after dropping off Grandma, we looked at each other in confusion. The list was done—no more people we had to see. By now we had both gotten used to spending the days in the car with a map and a sting of excitement. It was weird not to have a goal. Mia said what we both were thinking.

"What do we do now?"

"Well . . . I have to get back to Dublin and have the new chemo in a few days, so it's time for me to get home to pack. You, on the other hand, are free as a bird."

The smile she gave me was a bit melancholic. "I guess it's time for me to go home, too."

I looked down at my knee and didn't say anything for a while. I'd known this day would come sooner or later, I'd just hoped for the latter. There was no way I could convince her to stay longer; it wouldn't be right. She had her own life to tend to, and she had already given me more time than she should have.

"I will miss you." Looking her straight in the eyes, I could tell she was as sad as me.

"I'll come and visit again; next time maybe I can even bring Franz."

"I would love to see him."

She gave me a weak smile. "So let's go home?"

"Let's."

I leaned toward the car window while Mia backed up and smoothly turned the small car around.

CHAPTER 31
Dublin, Ireland, 2015

The break from treatments was over, and before I knew it, I was back in Dublin again. After the operation and six weeks of combined chemo- and radiotherapy, it was time for a stronger dose of chemotherapy. The medicine would be given as pills five days a month, and I thought it would be a piece of cake compared with having medication every day. What I didn't know was how strong the new pills were, with the capability to knock me out for several days in a row. Happily unknowing, I swallowed the first one on a Monday before I got into a cab and headed for the hospital. A new MRI scan was to be taken to see the progress.

On the way I felt a bit strange, but I told myself it was just a bit of motion sickness. I stopped typing on my phone, though, and looked straight ahead instead. When that didn't do the trick and the nausea increased in strength, I asked the driver to open a window. I leaned toward it and gasped for air like my old dog used to do when we had him in the car on a hot summer day. It seemed awfully stuffy in there, and I couldn't wait to get out of the car. I broke out in a cold sweat and reached for a napkin in my bag to wipe my forehead. When I saw the road signs indicating that the hospital was getting closer, I got a bit calmer, even though the nausea seemed to have risen slowly upward. I swallowed more often than usual, closed my eyes, and started counting backward from a hundred.

When the car stopped, I couldn't get out fast enough. Thank God for those apps that let you pay automatically with your card—I wouldn't have been able to sit one second longer in there, or manage to wait for the driver to give me the right change back.

I was late, but I couldn't go inside just then. It must have looked a bit weird that I just stayed by the main entrance without entering, but I needed the air. A few minutes later I took a deep breath and went inside, toward the radiology department. Apparently there was no need to stress: the waiting room was packed, which indicated that there were delays. I sat down on one of the sofas, next to an old lady. By now I could feel the sweat starting to pour down my back, and I did my best not to draw any attention, even though I believe my loud breathing seemed a bit strange.

My tactic lasted exactly four minutes. I know, since I'd kept a close eye on the clock on the wall. When I realized I wouldn't make it till five, I rose up briskly and ran toward the bathroom, where I just managed to lean over the toilet before a cascade of my breakfast and most of last night's dinner poured out of me. There was no time to lock the door, and I thanked my lucky stars that there was no one in line. It's bad enough to feel sick at home, and much worse to experience it in public. I sobbed for I don't know how long and fought the urge to return to the waiting room. I could not afford to miss my appointment, but I didn't trust my stomach just then. After a while a nurse from the reception desk knocked on the door and asked me how I was doing. She must have seen my sprint and put two and two together. Parts of me were mortified and didn't want anyone to see me in this state, and parts of me were grateful she seemed to care. She calmed me down by promising I would still have the MRI; they would postpone it till I could at least stand up by myself.

When I returned to the waiting room, it felt like everyone was looking at me, even though it might just have been in my head. I couldn't hold back the tears and must have looked awful, with stripes of black makeup all over my face and a nose that didn't stop running. My head started to hurt and screamed for water, but I knew that wasn't possible. All attempts to ingest anything right then would have been catastrophic. The friendly nurse sat with me until it was my turn, and I couldn't remember the last time I'd felt so small. I could not tell my mom about this; she would have gotten straight on a plane to be with me, and I wanted to handle it on my own. I don't know why I was so stubborn, but I was used to being able to take care of myself and didn't like to ask for help. Looking back at what happened, though, I think it might have been wise to have let someone come with me—but then again, it's easy to second-guess.

Two nurses showed me to an annex outside the hospital where a machine was waiting for me. They told me that the hospital had just one stationary machine inside, and this one was used when they were overbooked. They both started to shiver and left as fast as they could. Two guys took over, and I felt sorry for them for having to work in the drafty environment. Even so, they seemed to keep up a good face. Their smiles disappeared quickly when I removed my wig and revealed the scar and some small wisps of hair that were still there. I tried to pretend that their reaction didn't hurt my feelings and went into a small dressing room to change into the unattractive hospital gown.

When I came back, I was placed on an adjustable table, similar to the one used in radiotherapy, only this one didn't force my head down as much. The technicians injected something into my arm, but I was too tired to ask what it was. They asked all the normal safety questions and made sure I was not claustrophobic, then pressed an awful lot of buttons. After receiving a small device to press in case of panic, I was slowly moved inside the big machine. I tried my best not to picture a cremation, but the similarities were striking. The noise the machine made can best be described as roadwork done by a big, loud borer. It drowns out any other sounds and drives all passersby crazy. They had given me earphones with some really bad country music to block out the noise, but it didn't help much. *Oh well*, I thought, *my ears shouldn't be the biggest worry right now.*

As the loud noise intensified, my tears started pouring out. In there no one could see me, and that was the relief I needed. It struck me how surreal the situation was: on a Monday morning, most of my friends were probably already done with their first meetings, heading for a coffee. How I wished I could be in their shoes! It took all of my willpower to convince myself that I was OK and that I would get out of this experience stronger than before.

The symphony of different drilling sounds continued for about twenty minutes before the table started to move slowly and they let me out.

***

In the cab on the way home, I prayed I wouldn't throw up—it would be not just gross but also extremely embarrassing. I sat in the front seat and didn't take my eyes off the road. The cab driver didn't seem to understand the seriousness of the situation and made small talk about the weather and the latest rugby game. I let out weak humming sounds to show I was listening, but I didn't feel well enough to take an active part in the discussion. My whole being was focused on preventing another accident that day, and I was barely aware of what he was saying. Miraculously, we arrived at my apartment, and I left the car with lightning speed, heading for the elevator and my safe bed.

The rest of the day was spent moving back and forth to the bathroom while counting the hours until I had to take another pill filled with poison. I knew I had to find a way to keep the pills down; otherwise I would be in real trouble. Life is filled with surprises: if anybody would have told me a few months earlier that I would be lying in bed hugging a teddy bear my mom had gotten me, I would not have believed him. *Well, I guess you should never say never*, I thought and buried my face in the tiny stuffed bear's fur, crying in silence.

CHAPTER 32

A week later, I found myself at the hospital in Dublin again, in the very same waiting room as before. It was time to see the doctor and to look at the latest scans, to see if the treatment had helped. My mom had insisted she wanted to be there and had booked her flight over. I was happy to have someone with me, even though she didn't seem to be able to calm herself or me down that day. She kept crossing and uncrossing her legs while nervously biting her nails. I felt a sudden need to bounce my knees up and down, a movement that I hated when others did it. Now I couldn't help myself, and I tried to do it as quietly as possible. The oncologist's voice echoed in my head: "Please bring somebody with you." When they specifically ask you to bring a supportive family member or friend, it can't be good news. I rubbed the back of my neck before I went up to get some water. This waiting made me crazy. Time would have passed faster if we would have talked, but my lips were pressed tightly together. I wondered if this was how criminals felt before they received their conviction. I hoped I would never find out.

"Miss Larsson?"

The soft female voice belonged to a petite nurse, who showed us into a room around the corner. At first she told my mom to wait in the waiting room but quickly changed her mind when it caused a scene, my mom arguing in a loud voice that made some nurses passing by turn their heads. I formed an "I'm sorry" in the air to the poor nurse, who'd probably just done as she was told. Dr. O'Brien was sitting behind his desk with his eyes glued to the computer, but he got up when we came inside. A second nurse joined us, which justified my misgivings that something wasn't right. Normally I met the oncologist by myself, and I couldn't understand what the two of them were doing there. The small room made me feel trapped, and it didn't help that the three of them looked at me at the same time without even a trace of a smile. My mom and I sat down in two chairs in front of the desk. I nodded to say hello, but I couldn't get a word out. Dr. O'Brien spoke first.

"Anna, how are you doing?"

"OK." It wasn't a lie. When I wasn't on chemotherapy, I felt pretty good, even though I had a daily sense of fatigue. All in all, nothing I couldn't learn to live with.

"I'm glad to hear it." Dr. O'Brien looked down at his papers, clearly not convinced.

"I believe you know that Dr. O'Connor, Dr. Cassidy, and I looked at the scans and have decided upon the next steps in the treatment."

I guessed it was a good sign that the surgeon, the oncologist, and the radiotherapist were all communicating, but most of all I wanted to hide my head in the sand like an ostrich. I had to force myself to keep looking at him. Dr. O'Brien went on, unaware of my internal struggles and lack of answer.

"I'm sorry to tell you that the scans show a second tumor."

My mom started crying uncontrollably next to me, and I wished I could say something to make her feel better. I felt dizzy but took her hand while the questions piled up inside of me: Was he serious? After all these treatments? I had accepted that I had a tumor, I'd even learned to say the word "cancer" out loud without getting the creeps—but this? What were the odds of a second one? A strange tiredness came over me, and I had to grab the armrest. Dr. O'Brien had the best poker face I had ever seen. He didn't even blink and continued as if we were talking about the weather and deciding whether to bring an umbrella or not.

"Dr. O'Connor doesn't want to operate on you again. You see, this tumor is placed differently, and there is a risk of you losing your vision completely in a new surgery. Dr. Cassidy says it's too dangerous to give you more radiation than you have already received . . . which leaves it to me. Unfortunately, we don't have many options. There are not many efficient drugs for this diagnosis."

I stared at him, fascinated by the fact that he had just taken his calmness to a new level.

"So . . . what are the next steps?" I knew I had to ask, even though I didn't want to know the answers. I looked at the door . . . What if I just got up and left?

"I suggest we give the chemo you are currently under for a few more rounds, then have another MRI. If the growth of the tumor is not slowing down, we will start a new medication. It is given as injections, so you would have to come to the hospital more often."

Short and concise. I looked at his left hand and the thin silver ring he wore. I wasn't surprised by his manners any longer; I just hoped he'd shown some more feelings when he proposed to his wife.

"And if that doesn't work?" It was like someone else was asking all the questions; the only thing that made me realize it was me was the fact that my lips were moving. The silence that filled the room was unbearable. The nurses didn't move an inch, and I was surprised to see Dr. O'Brien show a hint of sadness. His forehead formed deep wrinkles before he finally opened his mouth again.

"Then there is not much more we can do. I'm sorry, but it doesn't look good."

I wanted to scream or, even better, run. I glanced at the door again and couldn't wait to get out of there. The air seemed thicker, and I felt pushed into a corner I definitely didn't want to be in.

"How does that make you feel?"

His sudden interest in my well-being was sickening, and I just stared at him. What did he expect me to do or say? Burst into tears? Scream? Entrust him with my inner thoughts?

I felt I couldn't behave much longer; my boundaries were stretched, and I felt my face turning red in anger.

"I'm not happy about it, but I'll be OK." When he didn't stop looking at me, I got even more annoyed.

"Are we done here?" I stood up and tried to shake some life into my right leg, which had fallen asleep.

"Yes, just make sure you get a new appointment from the receptionist." He seemed relieved when he shook our hands. My mom was still crying, and the two of us couldn't get out of the office fast enough. Together we made a new appointment and walked out to call a cab. My mom had to take only one look at my face, and she then swallowed what she was about to say. We went home in silence—even when I started crying, we didn't exchange a word. She hugged me the best she could from her side of the car and rocked me from side to side to make me calmer. Whatever she did helped, and I don't know what I would have done without her.

***

Two days later, I saw her off at the bus stop that would take her to the airport. After the news, she had offered to stay longer, but her flight was already booked, and I didn't want her to miss it. When she protested, I told her I would be fine sooner or later, I just needed a bit of alone time to gather my thoughts. "Sooner or later." That was an interesting saying, when you thought about it—we always say that time heals, but the truth is that sometimes it doesn't. Apparently, I still had a long way to go before I could fully accept what had happened.

When the bus arrived, I helped her with her bag, and she got on reluctantly.

I don't know how long I stood by the bus stop, but several buses came and went before I slowly turned away.

CHAPTER 33
Sweden, 2015

What do you do when a reality you never wished for slaps you in the face over and over again? Normally, I would probably have booked myself a boxing class or a trip to a sunny place. But since my body wasn't strong enough for exercise, especially not with the upcoming treatments, these things weren't an option. I desperately needed to get away, though, and decided it was time to move back to Sweden. I had no clue when I would be able to go back to work, and while I waited, it would be easier to go through everything with my family close by.

Back in my parents' home, the days passed, but something was different. At first I couldn't pinpoint what was wrong, but I had a strong feeling I had experienced it before. I felt terribly empty inside and didn't feel like talking to anybody. I was perfectly happy to stay in my bed the whole day, even though my mom tried to convince me numerous times to get up. She cooked my favorite dishes, left small gifts on the nightstand,

and invited me to come with her on walks. When nothing worked, she gave up and let me be, hoping that I would come to my senses sooner or later. For a few days I became a person I despised, indulging in my own misery and feeling sorry for myself. My logical side told me this was just a reaction to the latest news from the oncologist mixed with the fact that the only one who understood me fully was hundreds of miles away. This new dark hole I was in seemed to block any signs of logic and common sense.

During these days, I didn't cry or scream. In fact, I didn't make a single sound. You don't have to be a psychologist to understand that my way of dealing with the situation probably wasn't the best, but I couldn't help myself. On the fifth day of being locked in my bedroom, someone knocked on the door. I didn't even move my head from the pillow or make an attempt to get up. The door opened slowly, and my mom came in with the telephone.

"It's for you." She left quickly after giving me the phone, obviously hurt that I hadn't let her in earlier, even though she'd only wanted to help.

I hesitated a few seconds before I cleared my throat and reached for the small device.

"Hello?"

"Sweetie!" Jasmine's voice bubbled over with positive spirit as always, and I could almost certainly tell she was smiling on the other end. There was noise in the background, and I believed she must have been calling from the office. She went on. "We miss you! When are you coming back?"

If I'd gotten paid every time someone asked me that question, I would not have needed an insurance company to pay for my hospital bills. Usually I answered "soon" and changed the topic, but now I wasn't sure I would ever get back. My silence said it all, and her voice got softer.

"You know I only ask because I miss you to pieces."

I still couldn't say anything, but she must have heard I was close to tears. I could hear her move to a quieter area, and her voice became serious.

"What's the latest? It's OK if you don't want to talk about it, I'm just worried."

I sighed deeply, and then told her everything, from the fact that so far nothing had helped to my decision to move the treatments to Sweden. My voice was a bit rusty after not having used it for a few days, but she waited patiently for me to find the right words. When I was done, she didn't say anything at first. I felt advice was on its way, and to be honest, it couldn't hurt.

"You need to let go."

"What do you mean?"

"Well, right now you have let so much negativity into your thoughts. It doesn't help you."

Easy for her to say, I thought and pulled the duvet closer.

"You can choose to focus on the good or the bad news. It's your choice."

Damn it, I knew she was right. That was usually how I tried to live my life—what had gotten into me?

"Speaking of . . . I have good news for you!" Her voice got light and bubbly again, like a child who couldn't wait to show a painting to her parents. "So I did a bit of reading on the latest cancer research when it comes to brain tumors."

Here we go. I had intentionally stayed away from searching too much on the subject, since all the statistics were not exactly motivating.

"Did you know that only about twenty-five percent of the chemotherapy you receive can reach the brain? Apparently we all have something called the 'blood–brain barrier' that protects the brain and makes it hard to treat brain tumors. Well, guess what?"

I had never heard about the blood–brain barrier before and wondered why my oncologist had not given me this information. I felt the panic rise inside me and decided that it was probably because it hadn't been scientifically proven yet.

"Scientists have found a way to break through the blood–brain barrier!" Jasmine almost shouted, and I had to hold the phone away from my ear for a second.

"What do you mean? How?"

"Well, it's awfully technical, and I don't know the details, but that's not the point. What we should focus on is that your oncologist is wrong. It is never too late, even if the medication you are on now won't work. Research is moving forward."

I let the news sink in. She was right, this was big. A small seed of hope started to grow inside me, slowly but steadily.

"OK, sweetie, I need to go back to work, but I'll call you later, OK? I will send you some articles I have regarding health and cancer."

We hung up, and I swung my legs over the bedside and stretched out my arms. Enough with the self-pity—it was time to start living again! I went to the kitchen and made a cup of tea. What had gotten into me? This wasn't like me; I usually looked on the bright side no matter what, and I got mad at myself for letting things that were out of my control affect me this way. I crawled up onto the windowsill that overlooked the garden. I had always loved that it was strong and spacious enough to sit on, even though I had to move a plant to be able to get fully comfortable. The heat from the cup warmed my hands, and I peered toward the bright sun.

I went over the past few days in my mind, trying to figure out what exactly had pulled me down. Of course, there were the obvious reasons, but when I dug deeper I realized there were other issues, too, that I had to work through not to get to the same low point again. I slid down from the window to grab a pen and paper. It would be easier to write everything down; that way I could go back to the notes later. I wanted to make sure I did everything I could to avoid falling into the dark hole of my mind again. After some time chewing on my pen, writing something down, then striking it and writing it again, I came up with two truths that I decided to live by:

1. Focus on what you can control.

One of the reasons I felt so low was that the situation was a lesson in control or, more precisely, the lack of it. It bugged me that nobody could tell me how the situation was going to end, no matter how many times I asked. Nobody could tell me if the new medication would work, if I would die within a year or live long but be on medication for the rest of my life. Nobody could tell me when I could get back to work and put this nightmare behind me. Before these thoughts pulled me down again, it struck me that the situation wasn't that much different from everyone else's. All of us are given one life, and we are free to form it the way we like. Nothing is for certain; we never know how long a journey we have, and we have to get used to the fact that it is out of our control. What we can control, however, is how we spend the precious hours that make up our day, and make the most out of it.

2. Don't look back, and not too far ahead either.

The second thing that was bothering me was that I kept on looking back at my life the way it used to be, and when I compared it with my life now, I almost always became sad. A piece of me still wanted to travel like my friends, advance in my career, attend crazy parties, and meet new people. Another piece of me realized that I had to forget that type of life for now and embrace what I had instead. In many ways I was wiser now and happier than I had ever been. Small things didn't bother me anymore. My jaw got tight when I thought of how obsessed I used to be with my career. Just the thought of not meeting a deadline had given me the chills, and if I had to go to an event with old classmates, I would sweat over the fact that some of them might have gotten further up the career ladder than I had. Now I couldn't care less. The realization made me feel freer than ever before, and my only regret was that I hadn't realized it sooner. I thought about the last time I had seen my colleagues. After a while, the conversation had turned, as always, to the future and where to go next. Nowadays it felt like everybody had a five-year plan in her back pocket. I used to be a part of these discussions, trying to decide what the smartest move would be. Now I realized that my horizon was shorter: I planned a week ahead, and even that was a stretch. I didn't see the point anymore of striving for something new before I had explored everything right where I was at the moment.

I leaned my forehead against the window, overlooking the beautiful garden. One thing was certain: everything had changed. I was aware that I might not live forever, but right then in that very moment, I was alive. Life happened; it had hit me with all its beauty and sorrows, and I wasn't prepared. But then again, are we ever? The days will pass whether we like it or not. We might as well smile at life no matter what it throws at us—eventually, it has to smile back. We all have a choice, and I choose to fight.

ACKNOWLEDGMENTS

I would like to thank everybody who made it possible to write this book. Without you, it wouldn't have gotten published, and I am forever grateful for the opportunity you have given me.

I would also like to give a special thanks to:

My mom, who has been by my side every minute of this roller-coaster ride. Your strong will pays off, and I could not have done this without you.

My dad, sister, and brother—you guys are the best, and I miss not having you closer.

Terese, for your inspiration and honesty. *Jag älskar dig.*

Can, for completing me. I am grateful every day for having you in my life.

All of my friends, because you are awesome! A special thanks to my roommates, for being there when things got crazy.

Fiona, who has been there all the times I needed encouragement and a push in the right direction.

Bob, for making me laugh even in the hardest of times.

Rebecca Hendry, my wonderful editor, who helped me with great ideas and advice.

Xavier Comas, my talented book cover designer, who creates magic.

Lisa Larsson, photographer and owner, GRAFIT DESIGN, for taking my portrait.

Quill and Inkshares, for great platforms and professionalism.

ABOUT THE AUTHOR

Caroline Reber works as an account strategist for Google and is based in Dublin, Ireland. She is originally from Sweden and graduated from the Stockholm School of Economics in 2013. After being diagnosed with cancer, she decided to fulfill her childhood dream of writing a novel. Through her writing, she hopes to inspire others to value their everyday lives and to keep a positive mind-set through even the hardest of times. Fifty percent of all profits generated from *Life Happens* will be donated to the Irish Cancer Society.

LIST OF PATRONS

This book was made possible in part by the following grand patrons who preordered the book on inkshares.com. Thank you.

Anders Reber
Anna Olejnik
Aurora Vintilescu
Can Ekim
Cecilia Li
Christina Andreasson
Eli Huzar
Emmy Jeanrond
Hilkka I. Eskelinen
Ines Clariana
Karin Rydberg
Madeleine Reber

Maria Mercedes Gortazar Yba
Maria Olander
Marie Dacke
Mutlu Balman
Rickard Nyberg
Robert J. Lutz
Sofia Clariana
Therese Reber
Tomas Bodin
Tord Ström
Yi Zhang

Quill

Quill is an imprint of Inkshares, a crowdfunded book publisher. We democratize publishing by having readers select the books we publish—we edit, design, print, distribute, and market any book that meets a pre-order threshold.

Interested in making a book idea come to life? Visit inkshares.com to find new book projects or to start your own.

CPSIA information can be obtained
at www.ICGtesting.com
Printed in the USA
FSOW01n0625081216
28065FS